by

C. P. HAZEL

CHIMERA

Sashay published by
Chimera Publishing Ltd
PO Box 152
Waterlooville
Hants
PO8 9FS

Printed and bound in Great Britain by
Cox & Wyman, Reading.

This book is sold subject to the condition that it shall not, by way of trade or otherwise, be lent, resold, hired out or otherwise circulated without the publisher's prior written consent in any form of binding or cover other than that in which it is published, and without a similar condition being imposed on the subsequent purchaser.

The characters and situations in this book are entirely imaginary and bear no relation to any real person or actual happening.

Copyright © C. P. Hazel
first printed in 2000
reprinted in 2006

The right of C. P. Hazel to be identified as author of this book has been asserted in accordance with section 77 and 78 of the Copyrights Designs and Patents Act 1988.

SASHAY

C. P. Hazel

This novel is fiction – in real life practice safe sex

How long had she been locked in the stocks now? How long since the two hateful women had left her alone? Tears filled her eyes and meandered down her cheeks as loneliness gripped her heart, and thoughts of poor Kiki being taken away again filled her with fear. Would her friend survive without help? Would she ever see her again?

Her eyes closed...

Chapter 1

It was dark — frighteningly so. Walking through backstreets of a city she hardly recognised, she fervently wished she hadn't left the party before her friends. And she had probably taken too much to drink as well. The narrowness of the ancient streets retained the heat of the day and made sounds travel in a disconcerting way. Voices and footsteps appeared very close, although once she had turned the corner there was nobody there. It was a feature of the strangeness that she found herself in that these noises had no physical presence. So it should have come as no surprise when the reverse was also true.

A figure was walking beside her. One minute she was alone and the next there he was. He stared ahead as if unaware of her presence. The girl was scared to say anything, and she was also anxious she might disturb him out of his reverie.

He was grey-haired, dressed in a tunic and trousers, almost like a uniform. Something flashed in the warm darkness and caught her eye. Glancing swiftly, she took in more detail. His tunic sported braiding around the sleeve cuffs and the hemline at the front. She assumed he was some kind of official. Maybe his duty was to escort lost visitors to their destination.

She hoped so, for lost was surely what she felt at this very moment. Where was she going to anyway?

'Mademoiselle will come this way?'

He paused and opened a large iron door.

'Oh, thank you. What's behind the door?'

'You are to learn to dance here. That is what has

been arranged, mademoiselle.'

He spoke softly, entreatingly almost, and the girl felt no alarm. She had always wanted to dance well. She stepped over the threshold and found herself in an archway lit by a hissing gaslight.

Emerging at the other end she found herself confronted by an elaborate frontage of tall windows and columned porticoes from which only the faintest light emanated. The sound of crickets from a garden nearby made the change from the street she had just left appear more dramatic than ever.

Before she knew it she was up the steps, in through the main door and along a corridor. His voice came from right beside her even though she hadn't been aware of his company.

'Here is the place where mademoiselle will learn.'

An open doorway to her right framed a dull glow of light. The girl went in and found it was darker than she had expected. She couldn't see the walls. She could only sense it was a large room, but was she alone here with the soft-spoken official?

There was music playing softly in the background, a waltz she thought. Her guide took her arm and escorted her to what must have been the centre of this room.

'Now you will learn to dance. It will be almost effortless if you do exactly as I say.' He spoke more loudly over the music. 'You must undress here. Leave your clothes in a neat pile. No one will see you. It is important for the influences that must enter you. Believe me, mademoiselle, you will be transformed.'

The girl put down her shoulder bag and peeled off her T-shirt and bra. What a relief to strip off and feel the velvety night on her skin. She sat on the floor to remove her shoes and jeans. She stood up again, dressed only in the briefest pair of lilac tanga pants.

Would she or wouldn't she? Where could be the harm, since she had taken off everything else? She slipped them off and dropped them onto the pile.

The guide took her hand again and drew her further into the room. The floor felt smoothly polished. At that point a bright overhead beam bathed her in a cone of light, cutting off her view of the immediate surroundings like a lace drape. The music became louder and more strident. The official stepped back.

'A mazurka! Now feel the rhythm. One two, one two three!'

And she did feel it. An invisible force seemed to be moving her body to the rhythm of the music. She felt exhilarated, literally swept off her feet.

As the girl relaxed into the sweeping rhythm of the music she looked around her, and to her pleasure she saw her own reflection. And not once but many times in the mirrors that now glowed with the image of her figure moving gracefully in the silvery light.

'Now a polonaise, mademoiselle! Be ready to spring to the music!'

She was dancing so wonderfully. She could feel that a man had taken her in his arms, even though he wasn't really there. Or was he? Occasionally in the mirrors she thought she caught sight of a figure dancing with her. He was dressed in a fine uniform with silver epaulettes while she, of course, was naked. She spun around until she became dizzy and couldn't trust her eyes.

Suddenly the music changed. Instead of being dashing and joyful, it was dark and tragic. She couldn't dance to this. The dashing young soldier had disappeared. Suddenly she was aware that all around, outside the circle of light, there were figures advancing very slowly towards her. For the first time she felt very naked. Then to her horror they began pointing at her, their hands entering one at a time into the cone of light. She felt threatened and frightened.

Then there was the voice of the ever-present official in her ear. Only this time his tone was no longer soft and reassuring. He rasped, 'Remember, this one is forever! For ever, mademoiselle!'

Natasha woke up with a start, her heart pounding. It was a nightmare, thank God, the one she had experienced before. She was as sure of it as it is possible to be. That final line she had heard.

'Remember, this one is forever!'

What did it mean?

She didn't want to spend time thinking about it right now. She would never get back to sleep again. She threw back the covers. Wincing as she swung her legs out of bed, she suddenly remembered what had happened last night. It just couldn't go on.

Wrapping herself in a towelling robe Natasha prepared to face an unseasonably bright autumn morning. She must be decisive, she told herself again as she took a cursory look in the mirror.

She still liked what she saw. Her high cheekbones and oval eyes, inherited from her mother's Lithuanian ancestry, added intensity to her look. Her long dark hair was sleek and healthy. Opening the gown she had a brief glimpse of her full breasts, ripe with promise. It looked like the same body she'd had at college, but so much had happened to her in the intervening year. She felt under the robe to the back of her thighs and confirmed by a touch of her fingertips that they were still tender. She did not want to look, just yet.

Was it really a year since she had left Scotland? So why was she still living with Jim? The subject of her question lay on the bed, heavily stubbled and breathing stertorously, mouth agape with his upper teeth bared. At least they were real enough. By her reckoning, based on a relationship that was by now very one-sided, not much else about him was. As if her barbed thoughts had mysteriously entered his consciousness, he gave a sudden snort and opened one eye.

'Shit, what's the time?'

'Don't worry. You haven't slept through the radio alarm. For once.'

'Uhuh, so you're the bright and early one today. Just give me a few minutes, honeypot, and I'll make us some coffee.'

He cleared his throat of some troublesome phlegm with a raw hawk.

But Natasha's attention was entirely occupied by the prospect through the full-height landing window as she descended the stairs. The chief consolation of living with Jim was the view through this window. The growing strength of the sun promised a glorious day. Such colours; if only they could be captured in the fabrics she designed.

The house was what she would miss most when they broke up. An 18th-century customs house overlooking the dock, Jim had picked it up for a song due to its condition. The interior had been mercilessly stripped out to make three open-plan floors, supported by structural steelwork.

From the outside visitors saw it as lovingly restored Georgian gem. At ground level, occupying a whole floor, Jim had created a fashion showroom – he called it a gallery – antiseptically finished in stripped pine. There he displayed the latest fashion ranges from the factory. So the house was really combined home and workspace.

In the attic a dormered sleeping space, uncomfortably cramped for two, adjoined a small studio which Natasha was allowed to use. The first floor living space was the filling in the sandwich that kept them apart in their daily routine.

She entered the small shower space created under the roof.

As the robe slipped from her shoulders she checked with a look over her shoulder for the marks on her lower buttocks and thighs. Sure enough, there was still a broad area of angry red where a flurry of strokes with the leather strap had chafed the skin on her right side.

The after-effects weren't going to inconvenience her. She had taken worse from Jim recently. At first, moving in with him had seemed a wonderful proposition to one with no attachments and fresh to London. She had packed up and left the flat she was sharing with Kiki without a moment's hesitation. But surely she should have seen how things would turn out. She towelled herself gingerly and went down to the kitchenette.

'How's that high-collar jacket shaping up?' He had stolen up behind her as she filled the coffeemaker. His sandpaper cheek rasped hers as she pulled away.

'So-so. I'll be working on it this morning and should get the patterns to the cutters by tomorrow.'

Why had it taken her so long to realise the passionate affair had become a 90s-style marriage of convenience. This was her way of paying her keep. Jim expected her to keep in touch with what was selling well in the high street young fashion shops and then produce a variation on the garment. It had to be similar enough, but not so similar that the retailer might sue Flirt for breach of copyright.

Flirt Fashion was the name Jim had chosen for his brand of teen and twenty fashion. She told him the name sucked and he should change it. But he reasoned he'd traded under the name for the past ten years and no one had complained. Typical of Jim, because he always preferred to stay with the familiar.

He would never take a chance with some really original design she came up with. To be exclusive was to be risky. That was the way his mind worked. He just didn't seem to realise that having something really original to sell might make him a fortune. Control freak, was how an observer might have categorised him.

If only it ended there, it might have been bearable. But in the last few weeks he had been taking his joint role as boss and lover just a little too far. The spankings were quite fun to begin with, but recently they had become too hard and too frequent. He had taken her consent for granted. And he would always go on for just that little bit extra after she asked him to stop.

In the morning light his face was lined, she noticed, not for the first time. Despite this Jim continued the attempt to look youthful by wearing his dark hair in a ponytail. Whatever had she seen in him? And why had he been so uncharacteristically impetuous in coming up to her after that charity catwalk show, where she had volunteered to model?

Jim, she had already discovered, was one of nature's true-born bachelors. Everything had to be done his way.

'Keep away from me this morning,' she snapped. 'If you must know, I'm not making good progress. It's a creative thing, so I can best handle it on my own.'

Sometimes, if he had an important buyer in he called her down to model the garments. That infuriated her too; it was as if he owned her body and soul both for work and pleasure.

With her hands full Natasha nearly stumbled as she ascended the open-tread chrome stairway. Pity she hadn't tripped, she thought. It would have been an excellent excuse for spilling the coffee on his head.

Was it already a year since she had come to London from Scotland? She thought back to the day when she and Kiki had arrived at Victoria on the overnight coach. It was a beautiful autumn morning, and there was so much going on, even at that early hour. She felt she could shout with joy.

How bright and exciting the world had seemed then! Anything was possible. This was the city where people quickly became famous and rich. Lots of Scottish girls had followed this same route and made it. They were both nearly twenty. So why shouldn't they, they thought as they stood facing each other, surrounded by luggage?

It was all due in a very roundabout way, to Ms Ailsa McGruer, the tutor on the fabric design course at the art college. She believed in administering a cold dose of realism to the first-year intake. She made it clear from week one of their course that they had all better clear their heads of fancy notions. Very few fabric designers made it in the fashion world. They would be much better off concentrating on furnishing and household fabrics. These would provide a steadier market for their skills. Brass tacks was her approach.

She was a severe-looking woman in her thirties, with her salt and pepper hair cropped short. She always dressed in designer jeans or trousers with few feminine touches to her clothes. Most of her students were women, and these were clearly favoured over the boys. She expected pure devotion from those whom she chose to favour with special attention.

Natasha had managed to rub along with her tutor until the end of the first year. It was the day of the shoot for the first-year fabrics show. A small group of the most favoured students had gathered in the forecourt of the college, made into a sheltered quadrangle by the new extension. The idea was to photograph the first-year fabrics against a natural background of grass and trees. The idea was fine for the furnishing fabric designs, but the fashion designers were expected to model their products.

Natasha had wanted to find another girl to model her creation, but others on the course persuaded her that she would do the job better herself. She was nervous partly because she was not happy with her body, and then there was the dress itself. She had become increasingly panicky at the thought of what she had to do. She was watching the photographer at work on the furnishing fabrics. These were unlike hers, made from good sensible materials such as canvas, calico or woven damasks in restful shades of blue and green.

'Natasha, it's nearly time for us to get changed.'

It was Leon, a short black boy, right beside her. He always made Natasha feel long and lanky, but she liked his easygoing ways. Leon had designed very ornate Elizabethan-style jackets with slashed sleeves, and he looked gorgeous wearing them.

'Leon, I'm quite uptight about this, aren't you? McGruer is not going to approve. She hasn't seen the cocktail dress yet. I offered to show it to her, but she smiled that tight little smile and said she thought it would be perfectly charming.'

'Is that the banana lace number? Well, since you ask, charming is definitely not the word I would have chosen.'

'You're not helping my self-confidence, Leon. The colour is soft sulphur, not banana. I do wish someone else were modelling it, though. Do you think it would totally spoil the effect if I wore a bra?'

'My dear, I think you should go for it au naturelle. The bra would quite spoil your vertical lines.' Leon made no bones about being gay, and she felt comfortable asking his opinion.

She was tempted to do a no-show when she saw the garment again in the cloakroom. It was so sheer it was barely more than a film, and the colour shrieked back at her in the mirror. But Leon's knock summoned her forth again. They walked out of the interior gloom of the corridor into the bright sunlight, and Natasha felt almost naked as she walked across the courtyard. So far no one had noticed the pair of them.

But then her luck ran out. From an open window on the top floor came a loud wolf-whistle followed by a raucous cheer. She looked up and saw some of the boys from the graphic design faculty, one of them with bright ginger hair. They were clearly determined not to miss this show.

At that point Ailsa McGruer looked up. Her face hardened and her eyes glinted, the invincible Presbyterian genes of her forefathers reasserting themselves in a flash of raw antagonism. Natasha forced herself to keep walking, aware of how all eyes were focused on what they could see beneath the film of daffodil lace she was wearing.

She looked briefly at Leon, who was grinning from ear to ear, enjoying the widespread attention he was attracting. In his dark purple jacket with the scarlet slashings and lace cuffs he looked a dish. It made her feel all the more under-dressed.

'Tell you what,' he said. 'We're like something out of Shakespeare. So, how about you Ophelia, me Hamlet?'

'Leon, what's the idea?' she asked. 'We're not going to start reciting Shakespeare. Not here, not now. Please don't say we are.'

'Okay, stay cool. Let's keep our heads. Could you try to be just a little mad, darling? How about humming a song under your breath and floating a little?'

'You're crazy, Leon. McGruer will pop her cork.'

'I'd say she'd popped it already. Let's go for it!'

Leon had always wanted to be an actor, she realised. He spouted on about 'Nymph in thy orisons', and 'get thee to a nunnery', while she floated around with her arms stretched out to either side. All Natasha could think of was Greensleeves. The group applauded as if it were a real fashion show and the photographer got to work, posing them against the trunk of the ash tree. Then someone produced a bunch of wildflowers and weeds and a few buttercups to go in her hair. It was like a relaxing dream.

But all dreams have their awakenings. The photographer was eventually satisfied. She had made Natasha lie on the lawn as if she were drifting in a stream. As they were packing up Ms McGruer beckoned her over. She wanted to see her in her room at lunchtime.

It was not a pleasant encounter. Natasha was told that her attitude left a lot to be desired, that her work was totally uncommercial and that if she wanted to make the grade next year she would need to learn to listen to what she was told and take instruction. Natasha protested, pointing out that they were there as students to use their imaginations too. But Ms McGruer was adamant. She must produce more commercial work or she would never get through the second year.

'Trained designers,' Natasha said. 'She kept on throwing the phrase at me. 'Fully trained', was how she put it. I felt like I was a performing seal learning how to spin a ball on my nose.'

Kiki snorted in delight at the comparison. They were sharing a drink in The Michelangelo, a pub with a walled garden that was only a few minutes walk from the college. The sun was hot and they sat out at a picnic table. It was near the end of exams, only a couple of weeks to go. The college crowd in stained and ink-smeared pants were noticeably in a majority.

'Tash,' Kiki said, 'I'm getting one hundred percent smegged off by the painting and drawing course. We're nearly at the end of the first year and I've hardly touched a paintbrush. It's all been still life and nature studies. God, I'll throw up till I'm dry if Calum Weir puts another Passiflora in front of us and insists we observe the parachute effect of the pistils.'

She made a tragic clown's face. Kiki and Natasha got on well together. Natasha had been attracted to the girl's friendly manner, even though she was actually quite vulnerable looking with her cropped hair and wide mouth. Kiki was from the north of England and shared a flat with two other girl students, whereas Natasha still lived at home. She was like the elder sister she'd never had.

'Kiki, I'm getting really depressed. Are you going on with it next year?'

'You mean the P&D? Well, it can only get better, can't it? God, what a thought if it got worse. Someone let me outta here!'

'What have you got planned for the vac then?'

'Nothing special. Just blobbing out at home and seeing some of my schoolmates in Barnsley. Suppose I could do some waitressing if my dad's not feeling too open-hearted towards me. You know, as in surgery.'

'But how about taking a year out? We could go anywhere: Tuscany, Morocco, India, the Andes. I just need to recharge my creative batteries. I feel I'm running out of inspiration and another year of McGruer would be a killer. She'd be delighted to see the end of me after today's carpeting.'

Natasha wasn't entirely sure which continent contained the Andes, but she liked the sound of them. And the idea seemed to have struck a chord with Kiki. She grabbed Natasha's wrist across the table.

'Tell you what, that's a wicked idea, Tash! Can't wait to see McGruer's face when you tell her. Why don't we start off in London? There are so many galleries, so many paintings and exhibitions! I've never seen a single one except in reproduction. Then we could head off across the channel to Paris, Brussels, Amsterdam. You name it!'

They both agreed they would ask for a year out from their course tutors. They spurred on each other's imaginations into wilder flight of fancy. Within a few weeks the world would surely be their oyster!

Chapter 2

'Natasha honey, would you come down for a minute?'

It was Jim's wheedling voice, so she knew she was expected to model for the buyers who had been downstairs inspecting the samples since nine-thirty. As usual, with no warning, she was expected to leave her drawing-board and come straight down to be a clothes horse. Swearing under her breath she slipped off the high stool and descended through their living quarters and a further set of open stairs which took her into the showroom.

Here the dividing walls had been removed, leaving a row of cast-iron columns and exposed metal beams, which the interior designer had painted in individual fruity colours. The effect, against the bare stone walls, was rather garish, but Jim thought it very post-modern. The samples hung on racks: dresses, skirts, some trousers, tops and jackets. They were lit by spots mounted on the columns and by the large arched windows that made the colours glow.

As she feared, the buyers were two middle-aged men, who both gave her lascivious looks as she walked in, plus the token woman who gave her a reassuring smile. Natasha knew the form. She was just the model. Jim never mentioned that she designed clothes. In fact, he hardly introduced her. She would go into a small curtained room next to the kitchenette and change. Then she had to walk up and down in front of the large wall mirror at the far end of the showroom while the buyers confirmed their orders.

They had only put aside four or five skirts and a similar number of jackets in bright citrus colours, which Natasha knew would go well with her dark hair. It shouldn't take too long. She swiftly scooped them up, returning the small dark-haired woman's smile, and headed for the changing room. Then she stripped to her underwear.

She usually paraded in front of them barelegged and barefoot. That way there was no possibility of creating a colour clash. It was an opportunity to show off her tan, too. But as she checked the hang of the first outfit in the mirror she noticed her ankles.

Although Jim had used the manacles on her before and the marks had faded quickly, last night he had decided to secure her to the stair rods by her ankles. She had protested feebly. The game had been Mutiny on the Bounty and she was dressed as usual in a sailor's outfit, mainly tight-fitting flares and her hair in a ponytail under a cap.

As usual she lay on the stairs, peering between the glass treads down into the showroom below. Although he turned the lights low, Jim made sure the flogging took place in front of the arched window, which only had a blind. She was sure that had anyone been looking up they would have seen the silhouette of a writhing figure under a flailing rope's end. Particularly when he suspended her by the waistband of her briefs.

And, to make matters worse, this time she had stripped down to a leather thong. When she sensed the handcuffs click on to one ankle and then the other she somehow felt more firmly shackled then usual. With her legs free she could at least kick back to deflect some of the strength of the lashes as Jim got into his stride.

This time he was laying it on harder, across her back and upper buttocks. The cords were quite soft, but she still felt a nip. It was as if he really needed to punish her. She couldn't move her feet more than a few inches. As she twisted round to protest she lost her grip and began to slip backwards before the manacles prevented her. She screamed as they bit into her, and quickly took the weight on her arms again.

She started pleading with Jim, who now stood above her and brought the cords down with a hiss, catching in her sensitive cleft. The bastard pretended to believe she was still in the game. He grabbed the back of her thong and held her just above the stairs. By the time he released her she was sobbing with the pain at her ankles. But strangely, a few minutes later she felt nothing, and they made passionate love on the showroom floor. In fact, it was the very floor she was about to walk out onto with the purple rings around her ankles plain to view. The skirts were knee length or shorter. Jim must have known she would have to reveal her marks. She pulled the curtain back angrily.

There were polite murmurs and Jim flashed her his weasel smile as she approached. Ignore them, she told herself, pulling up the jacket collar and giving the buyers a sideways come-on. She was just doing a job. Sashay, sashay, swing those hips and show them you don't give a damn.

Just as she was changing out of the final outfit there was a knock on the door and the small dark woman pushed her head round.

'Hope you don't mind me pushing in, my dear,' she said. 'But I very much wanted to have a word.'

Natasha smiled in assent.

'My name's Lucy Graves, I'm a group buyer for party wear. Nothing much here I was interested in, I'm afraid, but I was very impressed by you. Where did you train?'

'I trained nowhere at all. I've done one year of fabric and fashion at art college and we all modelled for each other, if you know what I mean. I never thought I was much good at it.'

'Au contraire. You're a natural, Natasha. That's an interesting name, too. Do you have East European blood in your veins?'

'My mother is from Lithuania, but my father was a Highland Scot. So I'm a bit of a mixture genetically.'

She tailed off, not knowing why she was being so confidential with a stranger.

'That's fascinating, my dear. Absolutely extraordinary. I'd like you to meet a friend of mine who is looking for girls who have something a little different to offer. Are you interested in modelling as a career?'

'Well, I thought I was going to be a designer, but I've taken a year off college and I'm just not sure at the moment. Do you really think she'd be interested in me?'

Natasha pulled on her jeans and faced Lucy fully dressed. The woman fished a card out of her handbag.

'Look, Natasha, I can't stay any longer to talk. Phone me over the next day or two. There's something coming up that might be just perfect. It's a charity fashion show to raise money for Anatolian disaster victims. We're staging it at our Piccadilly store and Astrid is supplying some of her girls as models. I know she's looking for one or two amateurs. Do you think you might be prepared to give it a whirl? Don't delay too long now.'

She flashed a dazzling smile and disappeared without waiting for Natasha's response.

Natasha's head was in a whirl. She felt like racing

after the woman shouting out that yes, of course she wanted to be a model – in fact she would go down on both knees and beg. But she restrained herself. She was twenty and knew a thing or two about the world, she told herself. If she rushed in with a quick answer they might take her for desperate because she had no other options. She would leave it twenty-four hours.

But first she must tell Kiki the news. There was no reply, but she left a message on Kiki's voicemail at her flat. She sometimes worked late waitressing in Soho, and would sleep right through to mid-afternoon.

Her friend sounded low when she phoned back.

'Tash, I wish you were back in the flat. This career beautician is really giving me the hump, you know what I mean?'

'Is this Babette? The one that moved in after the social worker left?'

'You've got her. The bathroom's off-limits for most of the morning and evening. We're talking serious hair sculpture and colour co-ordinated nails. It's dire. Luckily we don't run into each other when I'm on late at the taverna.'

'At least you can still see the funny side of it all. Kiki, let me know if Babette leaves. I'm still not really happy with Jim. It was a mistake. I realise it now.'

'Are you really going to leave? What ever will you do? I'll persuade Babette to leave, don't worry.'

'Well, wait a bit, Kiki. Look, I've got some exciting news. It may not come to anything, but this woman's invited me to take part in a charity fashion show next week. She's going to introduce me to a woman called Astrid who runs a modelling agency. She thinks she might be interested in taking me on.'

'Tash, that's wonderful!' Kiki enthused. 'I must come and see it.'

'I've not definitely agreed to do it yet.'

'So what's holding you back?' Kiki asked. 'Oh, don't tell me, it's Jim.'

'No, I don't think I'm going to tell him about it. I'm just... you know, apprehensive. I've only done those shows at art college.'

'But you were brilliant. You know you were. You've got the natural physique. You're just it, Sash. Go for it!'

'Okay, I will if you will.'

'You're flipping joking!' Kiki scoffed. 'They don't make clothes for midgets, unless the theme is Snow White!'

'Enough of that false modesty, Kiki. Come on, I need you for support.'

She phoned Lucy Graves after lunch the following day. She tried to stop her voice from betraying her anticipation, but it turned out even better than Natasha had dared to hope. Yes, she had spoken to Astrid Sunderstrom and she was keen to see Natasha on the catwalk, and Lucy would recommend Kiki. If she didn't get to model, at least she would be useful backstage. Natasha replaced the receiver and clapped her hands with delight.

Now, would she tell Jim? He was away on a trip to see suppliers in Greece and Turkey. That's what he had told her, anyway. Once she would have been invited too, she reflected. Natasha was tempted to phone the office to see if his secretary was there or whether she had accompanied him.

By the time Jim returned Natasha had definitely made up her mind. He had only phoned her twice, blaming the poor cell-phone coverage in the remote rural areas. As far as she was concerned, he'd been having a fine old weekend in Istanbul, a city she would have died to visit. Instead, Natasha immersed herself in her design work, producing a see-through blouse and skin-tight silver PVC cowboy trousers she knew Jim would never commission for production.

The evening he returned she made sure she got back as late as possible from a boozy evening out with Kiki. They were both keyed up with excitement at the prospect of the charity fashion show. Her high spirits were also fuelled by the Pisco sours Kiki kept ordering from a barman she knew.

'Really nice of you to be here to greet me,' Jim observed sourly as she let herself in after the third attempt. Hazily she noticed the remains of a takeaway pizza on the kitchen bar. She giggled. That would make him appreciate her attempts at cooking. Whatever the reason, he was severely disgruntled.

'Well, you should have phoned to tell me what time to expect you,' she countered. 'How was I to know?'

'I did tell you, a week ago, before I left. Did you have so many pressing engagements that my return slipped your mind?'

'No, Jim. I just thought you would be delayed.'

'By eight hours? It was a scheduled flight. And now it's nearly one o'clock in the morning in case you've lost count. Where have you been, then?'

'Out with Kiki. We went to a film and then had something to eat.'

The film was made up to account for some of the time they had in fact spent drinking. Oh God, surely he wasn't going to try the angry daddy routine again?

'You're totally out of control, Natasha. I ought to

give you a good leathering to sober you up.'

'Oh yes, I bet you'd love that. Did you get plenty of whipping practice with some compliant Turkish girl? I bet you did.'

She realised she had gone too far as he lunged out and caught her by the hair. Bending her head back, he brought his lips to her ear and hissed into it.

'What makes you think I've been doing that kind of thing in Istanbul? I was seeing sights of a different kind altogether, things you wouldn't appreciate in a thousand years.'

'Oh, who says? What do you mean? I probably know much more about Byzantine mosaics than you do.'

She realised she had fallen into his trap by playing the resentful teenager. Why couldn't she bite her tongue and showing some self-control? She knew what would come next.

'Even so, you're not too wise to have your bottom smacked,' he said. 'Come here.'

The wolfish smile on Jim's face betrayed his sense of eager anticipation. She just couldn't face the prospect.

'Jim, if you're thinking of putting me over your knee, don't. I shall probably throw up all over those expensive suedes. It was Rawalpindi lamb with spinach. So let's forget it for tonight, shall we?'

With as much dignity as she could muster Natasha draped her coat over a chair and went shakily up the glass stairs to the bedroom, tripping over the last one and jettisoning a slingback in the process. With a groan she pulled all her clothing off and snuggled under the duvet without bothering about taking off her make-up.

Bonhams was a fashion magnet for every well-heeled visitor to the capital. Its lavishly decorated windows appealed equally to veiled women from the Gulf States and high-maintenance Californian wives and girlfriends with a preference for skin-tight leather. Inside five floors dripped with gold leaf and carved wall panelling. It was an Edwardian stage set for anyone willing to indulge in as much rampant consumerism as they could afford – or even if they couldn't.

Haute couture was on the first floor, up a sweeping staircase into what could have passed for a small ballroom with mirrored walls. The catwalk was more of a stage, surrounded on three sides by gilded boudoir chairs.

Backstage, behind the curtain, there was apparent chaos as the five models prepared for first outfits, dashing in and out of the changing rooms, sometimes dressed, sometimes in their underwear. Natasha felt light-headed. She was introduced briefly to Astrid, a large ash-blonde in a Paisley-pattern silk kaftan, but there had been little time to talk. Everything was so new and exciting, it was difficult to concentrate on what she was saying. Her main impression of Astrid was her piercingly blue eyes.

But everyone wanted her attention and her approval for matching outfits and accessories. Her parting advice to Natasha had been, 'Chin up, my beauty, and swing those fine hips you have. Don't be intimidated by all the people. Remember, they are looking at the clothes.'

Even so, Natasha was very apprehensive. She still had no idea what kind of garments she was supposed to be wearing for the show. She was glad Kiki was there too, helping behind the scenes. The curtain was swished aside and there she was.

'Look at this, Sash. Unmistakably Alberta Ferretti apparently. What do you think?'

She held up a pair of crushed velvet boot-length trousers with frilled hems. She had also chosen a skimpy off-the-shoulder blouse held together with only one button. Kiki gave a saucy wink then took them out again before Natasha had a chance to say anything. She went to the next cubicle where Natasha knew there was a girl with chemically dyed hair and a ring through one nostril. She stood by her curtain surveying the scene. Only twenty minutes to go. Natasha prayed she wouldn't have to wear anything half so revealing.

She was hoping for something with more elegance. But she was being ignored while the other girls wandered around apparently selecting what took their fancy. Above the hubbub she could hear Astrid's strident voice taking snap decisions. She clearly expected her word to be taken as law.

The make-up girl had finished with her. She had doll-like cheeks embellished with gold sparkle. Kiki was supposed to be bringing her a beautiful embroidered and beaded jacket. Natasha had seen it hanging on a back rack, and had asked Kiki to choose a skirt to go with it.

Kiki did reappear next minute with the jacket, but she also brought the briefest mini Natasha had ever seen. It was made of pearl satin with a crimson appliqué pattern rather like flock wallpaper. Not exactly what she would have chosen herself, but time was getting short.

She quickly stripped to her underwear and slipped into the garments Kiki handed to her. Kiki looked odd, Natasha thought. She was quite calm for a start, as if this mayhem was her normal habitat. Maybe her waitressing job was a good preparation for all this hustle and bustle, Natasha reasoned.

'Well, what do you think?' Natasha asked. She twirled in front of her friend and looked over her shoulder in the mirror. It barely covered the critical area, and Natasha was unable to pull it lower over her broad hips.

'I think it'll cause a sensation, Tash, possibly even a riot,' Kiki enthused. She giggled, but straightened her face immediately. 'No, I'm dead jealous, to be honest.'

Kiki seemed a bit unfocused and swayed forward before catching her balance. This wasn't quite the morale boost Natasha had expected.

'Wish me luck, then,' she said.

Kiki gave her a peck on the cheek and hugged her. Natasha went over to join the other girls waiting at the curtain. They all seemed excited too, but they generally ignored her. The punk-style girl with the velvet-finish crop was peering through.

'Smegging hell, it's like the tube at rush hour out there,' she said. 'Standing room only.'

'Do you see any flashers, Chloe?'

Natasha's heart sank. The girl looked barely eighteen, almost unhealthily thin, with eyes made-up in a perpetual stare. A girl nearer her own age dressed in a beautiful sequinned chiffon gown came up to Natasha.

'You're the new girl, aren't you?' she said. 'I'm Saffron.'

Natasha didn't dare ask if this was her real or professional name. She had a cut-glass home counties accent, but was very friendly nevertheless.

'You're Scottish, aren't you?' the girl went on. 'You certainly don't look it.'

'We're not all carrot-haired and freckled, you

know,' Natasha returned. 'Sorry, I didn't mean to snap. I'm feeling nervous. Are there normally flashers in the audience?'

'Oh, no it's not that kind of flasher. Clare meant photographers, didn't you?'

A girl with long auburn hair, dressed in hot pants and crop top, gave her a smile. Further conversation was impossible because just then a stomping heavy metal track issued through the sound system, making Natasha's heart leap once more. All those people out there and she was about to make a fool of herself in front of them. Why ever had she agreed to this? She was after all, a designer not a model.

Saffron squeezed Natasha's hand in a comforting way. 'Okay, girls, it's time to go!'

The show passed in a blur. Each girl had four changes, but Natasha hardly noticed what she wore. Each time she went on she gained confidence. She realised all they could do to her was look. She didn't have to worry; she was in a different dimension of time and space. She wanted to pass again and again through that curtain to be the subject of so much attention.

The feeling of approval hit Natasha like a wave. The gasps and the applause, she felt, had to be for her. The expensive perfumes in the air made her head swim. The funky music brought out the feline in her and she felt confident enough to vamp it up a little.

And those flashes, like silent lightning.

Sashay, sashay. It was almost her name. Perhaps she was born to this after all. She tried to keep each step slow and controlled, becoming more aware of her hip movements as she walked. It was like swimming; buoyed up and floating on a tide of anticipation and applause.

For the finale all five of them went out with Astrid to a warm reception from the well-heeled audience. They had already paid five hundred pounds a head and still some women were handing over reservation cards to the sales staff with numbers written down. Clearly Bonhams were going to get plenty of business from the event.

After the show there was a buzz of wild relief in the changing rooms. The models were hugging each other as if one of them had just become Miss World. They included Natasha in their group. Maybe their previous reserve was due to her being an outsider. Natasha noticed the girl called Chloe was not joining in and sat at her make-up table chewing a nail.

'She's upset because Toni, the black girl, got to wear the suede skirt she'd set her heart on,' Saffron said, heading back with Natasha to the cubicles. 'Typical of Astrid to make a last minute change without discussing it. Chloe bears a grudge very easily.'

Suddenly there was a shriek from just outside Natasha's cubicle, and although only in her underwear, she stepped out to look.

'Let go of me, you vicious little weasel! It wasn't my fault! Let go, you're hurting!'

It was Toni, dressed only in a pair of floral print cotton briefs. She was being held by her hair as Chloe, dressed in skin-tight PVC jeans and a vest top, hauled her out of her cubicle and into the corridor.

'You knew that was my skirt, you bitch,' she hissed. 'You did it to humiliate me. Now it's my turn to make you look a fool.' She pulled the girl mercilessly over to a low settee put there for customers waiting to use the changing rooms. Toni,

howling in pain at her hair being pulled, removed
her hands from her naked breasts to try and relieve
the pressure on her scalp, and her nipples were then
openly on view.

Chloe rotated around the girl to sit down, pulling
Toni after her so that the black girl sprawled over
her lap. Natasha was wondering what Chloe was
planning to do next, when she noticed Chloe held a
hairbrush in her free hand. As Toni struggled to get
free, Chloe held her head firmly against the seat of
the settee beside her and began to strike the helpless
girl's backside. The sounds were evidence of an
unmistakably severe punishment and the girl's howls
confirmed it.

One hand snaked back to protect Toni's rump, but
it was given a warning tap with the hairbrush. With
her other hand Toni tried to release Chloe's grasp on
her hair, but the small girl had sufficient strength to
retain her implacable grasp. It was a shocking
display of unprovoked punishment, and it was over
as suddenly as it commenced. Chloe released Toni's
hair and pushed her to the floor, where she sprawled,
looking stunned.

At this point Astrid appeared and hauled Chloe
away, and she was not seen for the rest of the
evening.

Natasha was surprised at how she responded. She
felt sorry for Toni, off course, but not as sorry as
she might have. To have been switched herself, as
she remembered so clearly from last night, made her
realise that there were subtle links between pain and
pleasure.

The return home to Jim and the clothes in his
showroom was a letdown. She realised at a stroke
the huge difference between the mass-produced

garments she was helping to make and the haute couture market where every detail was dictated by a designer.

Astrid insisted that she and Kiki travel home in the black stretch limo Bonhams had laid on. It was close to two in the morning by the time they reached the harbour-side. Natasha realised such extravagance would enrage Jim still further if he happened to see it. And it would also blow her cover, as she had told him she was out for a meal with friends. With a bit of luck he should be tucked up in bed fast asleep.

Unfortunately for her Jim was very much awake. As soon as she'd let herself in she noticed, with a sinking heart, that he was wearing that special tweed jacket. And the Windsor chair was in the middle of the showroom. He was standing beside it with one hand on its backrest, just in case Natasha failed to notice its presence.

'Oh, hi there, Jim,' she said breezily. 'You shouldn't have waited up for me.'

In the distance she heard the soft purr of the departing limo. He would have heard it arriving and probably looked out of the window. She prepared herself to answer questions, and suddenly caught a glimpse of herself in one of the wall mirrors.

She was still wearing the dark denim dress with the flared profile she had loved so much. Lucy said she could have it as payment in kind. But Jim would surely notice it wasn't the same outfit she went out in.

'That's okay,' he said. 'I wanted to make sure you got home safely, Natasha. Enjoy your dinner?'

She nodded, and her gaze kept returning to the dark Windsor chair with its ornately carved spindles and curved arms. On the seat was a hank of white nylon cord.

'Besides,' he went on, 'I thought it would be fun to play a little game tonight.'

She sighed and reached up to the back of her neck to undo the zipper of the new dress, but it was a little stiff.

'Maybe I can help,' he offered. 'This is new, isn't it? Must have been very pricey.'

'I've been saving,' she said. 'Jim, do we have to do this?'

The dress dropped and she stepped out of it, and Jim's manner changed instantly. It was ludicrous, but Natasha felt her adrenaline level rise. Then Jim suddenly grabbed her by the hair and made her kneel with her elbows on the arms of the chair. She thought of Toni, and contrasted her own behaviour. She didn't feel the need to resist, and for some reason she wanted to be tied.

He took the hank of rope and skilfully bound one forearm and then the other to the smooth chestnut arms. Then he moved down and secured her thighs to the turned legs of the chair, just above the horizontal bracer.

She was securely pinioned at four points, forced to adopt an upright position. Looking over her shoulder she saw Jim cut the excess cord with a pocket-knife.

'That's better, young lady,' he said, breathing a little heavily. 'You'll find out that these days you can't just do what you like. There are limits on your freedom. So the sooner you learn this the better for you.'

While speaking he grabbed her hair again and twisted her head around to face him.

'Ow, you're hurting me,' she complained. 'Please let me go.'

'Not until you've taken your punishment, my girl,' he insisted.

Natasha noticed he'd folded the hank of cord, and it now resembled a lash with four tails. 'I hope you're not going to use that rope on me,' she said.

'Your hopes are due to be dashed, young lady,' he sneered. 'Now, where were you tonight?' She heard the rope lash sweeping the air and flinched in anticipation, but he was testing it against the chair-back in front of her.

'I'm asking you again, Natasha,' he said firmly. 'This is serious. I think you're giving me the run-around.' His face was a deep red at the strain of keeping his emotions in check. She suddenly realised how defenceless she was. The ropes made her one with the solid chair, and she couldn't move her arms or upper legs.

The swish behind her was the only warning that Jim had begun her punishment. She felt a smarting of the lower back area, just above the waistband of her panties. It jolted her into new awareness, but the cord was soft and the pain was slight. She twisted around and glared up at him.

'You pig!' she spat.

'Then tell me!'

She looked away, dismissing his demand. She knew what would follow, but she was strangely curious to see how much she could take when he was really angry. Jim grunted and she knew another stroke was on its way. She could play him along until it got too painful. But this time he lashed back and forth, so that the sensation of burning on her skin became cumulative.

'Stop it!' she wailed. 'You're going to mark me again!'

'Then tell me. Who were you really out with tonight? I saw you get out of the limo. Don't try telling me you hired it for yourself and Kiki.'

'Of course not. You are so stupid sometimes.'

'Then tell me who paid for it and who you were with.'

'Why should I?' she challenged. 'You don't own me.'

He must have seen red. She felt him grasp the back of her panties so that the material bunched in the cleft of her buttocks, and hauled her hips up as high as they would go. This time she received the lashing on her bare bottom and it made her gasp. Forehand and backhand, around a dozen times across her buttocks and lower back. Then just as suddenly he let her go, and she thought she heard a suppressed sob.

She strained to look over her shoulder and saw him, red-eyed, approaching her with knife drawn. He cut the rope at the knot and she wriggled free. Then she stood up and reached for her dress, and felt only a residual prickling on her skin.

'Despite the fact you're a sadistic bastard, Jim,' she said, 'I'll tell you what happened. You see this denim dress? Well, it was a gift from Lucy, the woman who came here last week – remember?'

'A gift,' he repeated suspiciously. 'What for?'

'For modelling at a charity fashion show tonight. Okay, get it? I've found myself a new career, and it doesn't include you.'

She swept up the stairs with new-found poise and locked herself in her studio with the duvet. Jim could make his own arrangements.

Chapter 3

Despite bedding down on the floor she had overslept. It was after midday. Suddenly it all came back to her; she'd had a real fall-out with Jim. She prayed he was away at the factory.

Natasha knew an awkward time lay ahead, as she had nowhere else to stay. And Kiki's flatmate was still in situ. As soon as she'd made coffee Natasha phoned the number on the business card Astrid had given her.

'Sundstrom Modelling Academy.'

She was through to Astrid, still as sharp as she had been at the show a few hours earlier. Natasha briefly explained her predicament.

'Quite okay, don't worry, sweetie,' the woman cooed. 'You're in luck. One of my protégées has just left to work with Calypso. We have a bed to spare.'

'A bed? You mean, the girls actually stay there?'

'You'll find it's quite a residence we've got here. Most return to their family at weekends, if they don't live too far away. We don't have any other girls from bonnie Scotland. They have to be eighteen minimum, but I usually like to get parents' consent if possible. In your case I guess we'll pass.'

Her Scandinavian accent mingled incongruously with a laid-back West Coast vocabulary.

'My father died when I was a child,' Natasha explained. 'I've lived away from home now for almost a year. So I can take care of my own affairs.'

'You will need to share a room with Saffron,' Astrid said. 'Is that going to be okay by you?'

'Oh yes,' Natasha agreed. 'We got along really well last night.'

'That's peachy! Why don't you visit tomorrow

afternoon then, and we can talk business? You realise you must sign up exclusively with me? Good, we'll strike a deal I'm sure.'

If anything, Astrid had undersold The Academy. The house was an impressive half-timbered mansion in a well-heeled suburb. It had its own front driveway behind a tall hedge; Natasha could see a side gate which must lead to a garden at the back.

Saffron had already revealed that classes took place in two large rooms with French windows opening onto a patio. The syllabus wasn't too demanding, consisting mainly of health and nutrition, basic French and Italian conversation and, of course, make-up and beauty tips. The physical education side consisted of gentle aerobics, deportment and dance. The main advantage the Academy gave its students was the chance to get experience of promotional and modelling work.

Natasha caught a glimpse of Saffron's blonde head through the mullioned bow window as she paid off the taxi. And sure enough, they met in the hallway. They air-kissed, and Saffron took her arm.

'How do you feel after the show?' she asked. 'You did so well. You're a natural.'

'Thanks, Saffron.' Natasha blushed a little. 'It was funny. After the first walk-out I felt hardly any nerves.'

Saffron smiled. 'Astrid said I was to watch out for you and show you around before dropping you off at her office. Do you want to see the room first?'

'I'm sure it will be lovely. It all looks so exciting to me, just like the setting for a country house murder film. Do you have cocktails on the terrace every evening?'

They shared the joke, but suddenly there was a loud shriek and Saffron made straight for a large panelled door to their left.

They entered a large airy room where three figures dressed in leotards were before the open window. Natasha recognised the crop-haired Chloe, who reluctantly released another girl's dark ponytail. A third girl in grey leg warmers leaned against a grand piano.

'Let's cool it, ladies,' said Saffron. 'This is Natasha. She's going to join the Academy next week. Chloe you must remember, Natasha. That's Jean with the ponytail, and Lesley.'

Natasha smiled at each one, but then she could think of nothing to say. She heard suppressed whispering as Saffron led her out, and suspected it was Chloe, who obviously had a spiteful side to her nature.

The two girls went up a spiral back-stair to the first floor. They followed a carpeted landing, then Saffron dramatically threw open a door, motioning Natasha to go in first.

She had an immediate impression of lightness. Sunlight streamed through the large window, illuminating a pale caramel carpet and darker matching bedspreads. The room was large enough to take two wardrobes, and Natasha was bowled over by its airy sumptuousness.

'It used to be the master bedroom,' Saffron explained. 'Astrid doesn't stay over now. I'm supposed to keep an eye on the protégées after dark. You could say that Georgette and I were their big sisters.'

Saffron stretched out luxuriously on the bed nearest the window. She did put on airs and graces but Natasha couldn't help warming to her.

'This one's yours, by the way. Just testing the springs for you.'

'Who's Georgette?' Natasha asked.

'Oh, of course. She left last week to join the Calypso agency. One of the Academy's star pupils. Astrid did well with a fat percentage of her earnings over the last six months, I don't mind telling you. Georgette was good. If I'd done half as well I would have got out too.

'She had already done a cover for Inspirations – you know, the monthly for secretaries. She should really make it big time, lucky bitch. You'll need to look closely at your contract, Natasha. Astrid will want to tie you up for six months at least, and then retain an option.'

'Tie me up?'

Both girls giggled. Natasha was glad Saffron was not the total innocent; being with Kiki had made her see risqué meanings in just about anything people said.

Saffron stood and moved close as Natasha opened her suitcase. 'Mm, you've got some nice stuff,' she said. 'I do so like your colour sense. I'd say we're about the same size... sorry, I'm being a bit presumptuous.'

'I don't mind,' Natasha said, 'and I can see you've got some fabulous stuff, too. I think I would get the better of the deal. Do all the other girls have wardrobes like this?'

'Depends on daddy. But then, I'm almost twenty, and I need to dress to impress if I'm going to make it in this game. How about you? Do you plan to go into career modelling?'

'I don't see why not.'

Saffron was standing close behind her. Natasha could feel her body heat and a faint musky scent.

'I love the way you speak, Natasha,' Saffron said, a little huskily. 'I'm told a Scottish accent really turns men on. Do you have a boyfriend?'

'Kind of... well, no, not actually.' Natasha tried not to appear flustered by the girl's close proximity and changed the subject. 'I'm sure I could stand it here for six months if there was a definite career awaiting me. Perhaps I should go down and see Astrid now?'

Astrid was seated behind an impressive desk covered with photographs. She had wire-framed spectacles perched on the tip of her nose in headmistress style. She stood and embraced Natasha warmly as if they were good friends.

'Natasha, my darling,' she purred, 'has Saffron done her duty and shown you around?'

Natasha beamed and nodded. 'It looks wonderful, Astrid. How many girls are here?'

'We have ten protégées boarding and a similar number coming in daily. So the joint is usually jumping. Today a bunch will be out on assignments.'

'Is that for photo-shoots?'

'Promotions, shoots, or semi-pro modelling jobs. You're still in the honeymoon stage, honey. It can become a drag, believe me, but here at the Academy we try to instil a professional attitude into our girls.'

'I'm really looking forward to getting some proper training,' Natasha enthused. 'What do I have to do? I've a little money saved, but it isn't very much.'

'First things first,' Astrid said. 'I'll show you our basic contract and you read it through before you decide anything. You agree to stay with us for six months and the Academy takes a percentage of your earnings. Obviously you won't gross much for the first few months, but that's the reason for a six-month agreement.'

There were two pages of dense typing to read.

What possible traps could they hold for Natasha? She looked briefly over the clause that related to her undertaking a six-month stay. If she failed to complete it she would be liable for the full cost of her bed and board. Something about contingent liability – whatever that was.

'Where does it say how much I have to pay for fees and upkeep?' she asked.

'There are no fees at the Academy. I hope to recoup the cost of each protégée from my share of her six-month earnings. In the case of most students whose parents are paying upkeep I would take twenty-five percent.'

'Oh, suppose I couldn't afford the upkeep costs?'

'Well, I did have this situation once before,' Astrid said sagely. 'It was with a girl of about your age. I calculated that her earnings would be higher. Even so, I had to take a higher percentage.'

'How high, for example?'

'I'd say we'd be talking fifty percent.'

'Wow! And how much would I need to pay for upkeep?'

'Nothing at all. Unless, that is, you leave before your six months are up. How are you placed for spending money?'

'I have a little in the bank,' Natasha confirmed. 'And there are one or two things I'm going to sell, so I should be okay.'

'Well, don't hesitate to come and talk,' Astrid said with a comforting smile. 'I'm sure we can arrange a loan. Speak to my assistant, Evelyn Marnie, if I'm not in the house. Okay, so does that answer all your questions?'

'Yes...' Natasha drew a breath. 'I'll sign right now, if you have a pen.'

'Just one more thing, honey,' Astrid put in. 'Are

you sure you want to become a model? It isn't the perfect life for everyone, you know. There's all the travelling and the long hours doing nothing very much. You gotta be really dedicated to see out the course. Once you start there's no time for second thoughts.'

'I'm serious, Astrid,' Natasha said determinedly. 'You'll see,' and she signed both pages of the agreement.

'I'll give you a copy with my signature on tomorrow,' Astrid said, taking the documents from her. 'When do you want to start?'

'Tomorrow?' Natasha suggested hopefully.

The blue eyes bored into her almost suspiciously, then Astrid's face relaxed into a smile.

'Of course, why not? We'll see you tomorrow at five o'clock.'

Natasha had done it! As Astrid had made clear, there was no turning back. She must pack up and leave Jim tomorrow, and that would be the end of it. What she would say in her farewell note she could not yet begin to imagine. It was terrifying, but it also made her dizzy with excitement.

She made a mental plan of how to make the escape. She could leave a few larger items like her design equipment and computer with Kiki. A couple of suitcases were all she could take with her. But it would mean jettisoning some of the dresses she'd picked up through her modelling work for Jim.

She phoned Kiki and gave her the news. Her suggestion was that Natasha should leave as soon as possible. Kiki would call round with her flatmate, who had a car, as soon as she got back from work.

It didn't take long to pack two suitcases, but then she saw a pale lime jacket, one of the few designs that she had actually persuaded Jim to put into production on a small run. She slipped it on and admired herself in the mirror. Yes, she must take that too. But where were the black pedal-pushers that went so well with it?

She was still looking when Kiki and Joan turned up, and she still hadn't written a farewell note to Jim. It would be rotten to leave without an explanation. To do that with any honesty required her to point out to him how badly he had treated her. He would be furious, but she wanted to help him take it as calmly as possible.

Then the doorbell rang.

'Are you ready to scram, Tash? God, you don't look it. Where's your stuff?' Kiki burst in past her without waiting for an answer. Then she stopped in her tracks, turned and whispered, 'Is he back?'

Natasha shook her head.

'Well, thank the good lord!' Kiki sighed. 'But we'll need to look sharp. This is Joan, by the way.'

The mousy girl dressed in a trouser suit smiled diffidently at Natasha, who thanked her for offering her car.

Natasha led Kiki upstairs where her prized possessions lay in a heap. Rather a large heap, as she now realised. Kiki took a sudden intake of breath when she saw it.

'Did you think we'd have the limo parked outside?' she scoffed. 'There's no way we can take all that, girl. Let's try the two suitcases first, and then we'll see what space we have left.'

There wasn't much. Only one suitcase would fit in the boot, but Natasha was determined to take her pattern books and small PC even if she couldn't fit in the drawing board Jim had given her as a present. She was already starting to feel sorry for him as she gave her wardrobe a last look; it was about half empty.

Then Natasha became conscious that a car horn was pumping out a steady rhythm outside. Looking down through the window she could see why. Jim's blue BMW had pulled up outside. He got out. She could see the small bald patch on top of his head, and at that moment he looked up and saw her.

Her legs started to quiver as the adrenaline began to course. She was only halfway down the stairs when Jim came in, and he immediately saw her handbag and a small heap of clothes by the front door. It only took an instant for the expression on his face to change to dark anger.

'So what's this all about?' he asked.

No need for the farewell note after all, she thought, her heart in her mouth. 'Hi Jim,' she managed. 'I – I'm really sorry it has to be like this, but I'm leaving you—'

'You were just going to slope off without telling me, then?'

'No, I was about to write you a note.' She knew exactly what he was going to ask next. He had adopted that foxy expression which she knew meant he thought he had her trapped.

'And just why are you leaving, Natasha?' he said.

'We just don't get on, Jim. You must know that. I'm too young for you. I need to go out and discover a bit more about the world. You just want to shelter me from anything new and unexpected. That's really sweet of you, but...'

She trailed off into silence. Giving him a smile, she moved to pick up her things, but he grasped her shoulder and pulled her upright.

'Oh no, you don't get out of here so easily, you little bitch!' he growled. 'You owe me more than that, Natasha. Who gave you a roof over your head for the last year? Do I get no thanks for it?'

'I – I didn't know you were expecting any, Jim,' she stammered. 'I thought you did it because, well, because you loved me. Silly me. Anyway you got pretty good value out of me with all those designs I did for you.'

'No, that's not good enough!'

He held her by the arm and she could feel his spittle in her face. Clearly she faced the possibility that he wasn't going to take this like a lamb.

'But I happen to think it is,' she said, trying to keep her voice level.

Just then Kiki's voice made him whirl around in surprise. 'Oh, I might have guessed,' he sneered. 'Your call-girl friend.'

'What did you call me?' Kiki demanded.

'Well, that's what you do between your waitressing jobs isn't it?'

Kiki flew at him with her talons out, but letting go of Natasha he caught her wrists and held them above her head.

'Let her go or you'll suffer.' It was the surprisingly authoritative voice of Joan, who had followed Kiki into the house. Jim turned his head in surprise at yet another interruption, and this was his undoing. With astonishing speed Joan grabbed the top of his ear, pulling his head back. He howled in surprise and pain, releasing Kiki's wrists. The mousy girl led him, at a half crouch and still bellowing, into the showroom. She brought his face up to a level with hers and put a finger to her lips.

'Now listen to me, you unpleasant little man,' she calmly said. 'Just accept reality. Instead of trying to take your anger out on others, take a look at yourself. You've enjoyed a year-long relationship with Natasha. She's still young and she wants to find out more about herself without having you breathing down her neck. You're just lucky she's not suing you for support. Think about it.'

Jim was listening with close attention, though his ear still remained in Joan's firm grasp.

'Now, I'm going to release you and we're going to leave,' she went on assuredly. 'If you continue to threaten us I'm calling the police. So just behave like a man instead of a spoilt little boy, okay?'

Jim clapped a hand to the side of his face and gasped with relief as she let go. He must have been aware of how ridiculous he looked, and suddenly Natasha no longer felt sorry for him.

Joan had said exactly what she should have written in her farewell note. She now realised how much more she had put in to the relationship than he had, and now she was looking for a change. If she embarked on a modelling career with Jim in tow she would always be torn by his demands. She was doing the right thing. She had to leave him.

Joan and Kiki dropped her off the following afternoon at the Academy. Kiki got out of the car and gazed up at the imposing black and white upper storeys, with dormer windows pushing up through the tiles like soulless eyes.

'Bejasus, this is some pile,' she said, screwing her nose up prettily. 'Do you really think you're going to be happy here, Tash? It's a dead-ringer for the place in that ancient Rebecca movie.'

'Kiki, don't put me off now,' Natasha sulked. 'It's something I have to try. It could be a watershed, so it's worth obeying a few rules and regulations. I just don't think I'm going to make it as a designer, so I want to try modelling, that's all.'

She kissed her friend and waited with her suitcases

as they drove off, waving. She had never felt so alone, and felt a lump forming in her throat.

When she turned she found a tall woman dressed in an austere grey business skirt and jacket standing in the doorway. Her black hair was scraped into a severe bun. She moved stiffly forward and shook Natasha by the hand.

'You must be Natasha,' she said. 'I've been expecting you. I'm Evelyn Marnie. Some of the youngsters call me Miss Marnie, but I think you should call me Evelyn.'

Her dark eyes scrutinised Natasha from head to toe. 'I can see what Astrid meant when she said you were something rather special,' she said in a dour tone.

'Oh.' Natasha blushed, uncomfortable with the unexpected and unenthusiastic compliment, and then despite her attempts to stop the woman, Evelyn picked up and carried one case into the hall. They went on up to the room she was to share, and Evelyn placed the case by the window.

'This is your bed, I understand,' she said.

'Apparently so, but how did you know?' asked Natasha, feeling a little uneasy.

'Saffron told me,' the woman explained. 'It's part of my job to know everything.

'She's gone to the movies with one or two of the other girls, but they shouldn't be back too late,' she went on. 'Did you know we have an eleven o'clock curfew? And, of course, no boyfriends or alcohol on the premises.

'Saffron is in charge when I'm not here. You'll find I do sometimes stop overnight; I have a little room in the attic. It's small, but it suits me...' her eyes glinted and flitted across Natasha's breasts. 'Perhaps you'd like to come up and see it when you've unpacked...'

And then Evelyn left her alone, and Natasha sighed with relief. The woman was a little creepy, but clearly a figure of authority in the house.

She found some empty drawers and unpacked, but the thought of Evelyn nagged on her mind. Was the invitation what Natasha suspected, or was she being oversensitive and the woman was merely being friendly? It was so difficult to know, but once unpacked and with nothing else to do, Natasha decided to risk it.

So she followed the twisting staircase again to the next floor, and then a further flight at the end of a musty passage, with only a skylight to help her see.

She climbed the few remaining steps and tapped softly on the door at the top. Evelyn pulled it open, and stood in the shadows with that disconcerting sparkle in her eye.

'I hoped you'd come up,' she said quietly, and Natasha had the distinct impression that she was expected. The woman indicated for Natasha to enter, and then closed the door with a soft thud that made Natasha wish she'd been less adventurous and stayed in her own room.

Evelyn had not exaggerated when she'd said the room was small. Apart from a single bed there was one armchair tucked in beside a small cast-iron fireplace, which was fitted with a gas fire. The other piece of furniture was a small table with an electric kettle on it. Natasha was offered a cup of tea and the armchair, and once the tea was made, Evelyn perched with back straight on the edge of her bed.

'Now,' she said, smiling inscrutably, 'tell me about yourself.'

Natasha gave her some highlights of her life in Edinburgh, and a bit about her life since arriving in

London. She left the Jim episode deliberately vague.

They talked for an hour or more, and Natasha began to discover a warmer side to balance Evelyn's businesslike approach. She sensed Evelyn was also an insecure person who would fall back on any status she could to bolster her self-esteem.

Then there were voices from below and footsteps along the passageway. Someone knocked on the door and Evelyn rose to see who it was.

'Ah, Saffron and Clare,' she said. 'Home at last. Are you searching for me or Natasha? Either way, your search has been successful.'

She stood aside slightly so the two girls could see Natasha in the armchair.

'We wondered if she was going to join us for supper, Miss Marnie,' Saffron explained. 'We're just about to start cooking.'

'I'm sure she will,' she said, with just a hint of regret in her voice. 'I'd better let you go, Natasha. Saffron, would you send Jean up here, please?'

In the basement kitchen two other girls were busy preparing a salad.

'Do you want to risk Clare's vegetarian lasagne or would you like something ready-made from the freezer?' Saffron asked, taking Natasha's arm.

Here was an opportunity to clinch a friendship. 'I'd love to try the lasagne,' she replied. 'Can I do anything to help?' She was handed a block of cheese and a grater by Clare.

'Where's Jean?' Saffron asked.

'Last seen heading off with Chloe to the twenty-four hour shop,' Clare told her, 'for their usual purchases.'

Meaningful looks were exchanged, but before more could be said the two girls under discussion were heard descending into the basement with snigger and giggles. Jean, her dark ponytail tied up with a yellow scrunch, carried an off-licence bag, which she half-heartedly tried to put behind her back. Then Chloe took the bag off her, and ignoring the others, strode confidently over to the kitchen cabinet containing glasses.

'Well, what are you lot looking at?' she challenged. 'You all know where we've been. It's been a hard day and we think we deserve a D, R, I, N, K. There, I almost said the dreaded word. Happy?'

'You know the rules,' Saffron said wearily. 'You take the consequences.

'Jean,' she went on, turning to the other girl, 'Miss Marnie wants to see you in her room before she goes.'

'Oh no, is she still here?' Chloe riposted dismissively. 'You'd better watch yourself, Pony. She'll be wanting to saddle you up again.'

Jean blushed and dashed anxiously back up the stairs. Chloe followed with two glasses, and Clare called out as she went, 'Tell everyone supper's going to be ready in half an hour!'

'What's wrong with Chloe?' Natasha asked, lying in bed as Saffron undressed. 'She seems to always be on the defensive – or is it attack?'

Saffron had slipped out of the cashmere pullover and skirt she'd worn for the cinema. Natasha discretely admired the girl's firm breasts tipped with delicate coral as she slipped a delicate nightie over her head.

'Well,' Saffron replied pensively, 'as you can see, she seems to need these fierce attachments. If you're not on her side then you're automatically seen as a potential enemy. So she always surrounds herself with a small group. It must be something to do with her upbringing, but I've never really felt like asking her.'

'Is she...' Natasha pursued carefully, 'well, into girls, do you think?'

'I can only surmise,' Saffron said. 'But let me put it this way; she's been through a string of roommates. They all ended up in a screaming match until eventually Astrid agreed to her having a room to herself. The only one who can control her is Evelyn. After she's been to the attic she's as good as gold for a while.'

Saffron slid into bed and gave a languorous yawn.

'By the way,' she went on, 'you'll have the room to yourself for a bit. I'm off home for the weekend. Mind you don't have too many orgies while I'm away.'

By the end of the week Natasha had begun to feel quite at home. It was nice to have the room to herself, if only for two nights. On Saturday morning she treated herself to some time with her sketchbook. It felt wonderful to do something creative again.

In the evening she met up with Kiki and a few friends who were all eager to hear how she was getting on. It was late when she paid off the taxi, and she realised she'd had more to drink than was wise.

As she opened the heavy front door she was greeted by a wall of music. The girls must have put the sound system in the dance room up to maximum volume. Above it she could hear an odd screaming, whether of pleasure or pain she couldn't tell.

Not knowing what to expect, she carefully pushed

open the door to the dance room.

Chloe was there, of course, with three or four of her cronies. And friendly Clare was also there, over by the piano dancing with Toni. It was covered with bottles and juice cartons. The air smelt sweet with alcohol, and probably dope.

At first nobody was aware of her presence, but then Chloe, smoking a joint, looked round with a lopsided expression and glazed eyes. She nodded to Jean, who turned down the sound system.

'So, just look who's here,' she said, with not a little effort to sound coherent. 'It's the new girl. Miss prim and proper.' She approached Natasha unsteadily, clearly in the mood for a clash of wills.

She was wearing cherry-red PVC trousers and a crop top in clashing tangerine. She had a gold star in her navel. The others had also made an effort to dress up a little, with party clothes and body jewellery.

'Is – is the party for anyone special?' Natasha asked cheerily, trying to defuse any nasty situation that might arise.

'Yeah,' Chloe slurred, 'it's for you, new girl. We were just waiting for you to turn up. Want a drink?'

What should Natasha do? If she refused she would just antagonise Chloe further. 'Okay, thanks,' she beamed, although she wanted her bed. 'Can I have a glass of juice, then?'

'Totally out of juice, aren't we girls?' Chloe sneered. 'So you'll have to make do with gin, okay?'

There wasn't much Natasha could say as she was handed a tumbler, so she took a sip, and it was definitely neat.

'Come on, new girl,' Chloe goaded. 'Let's see you drink it all down.'

She took another sip, and then another. Chloe's

group was gathering round in an increasingly menacing way. Natasha noticed that Toni and Clare had edged towards the door, her unease increased and she took another quick gulp of the spirit.

'I think it's time for the initiation,' Chloe announced.

Natasha didn't like the sound of that. 'What... what initiation?' she asked, wishing she hadn't.

'It's to test your willpower,' Chloe informed her. 'Most important if you're to have a successful career in modelling, don't you think?'

The neck of the bottle of gin chinked on the lip of Natasha's glass and poured an unwanted refill.

Chloe took a deep drag on her joint and squinted at Natasha through the smoke haze expelled through her nostrils. 'So,' she went on, 'get your clothes off, and we'll begin.'

'I... what are you going to do to me?' Natasha asked.

'Just get your clothes off and you'll find out, won't you?' Chloe giggled, and her entourage giggled with her.

'But—'

Natasha tried to object but Chloe's patience suddenly snapped. With a snarl and incredible speed her lips engulfed Natasha's and her tongue snaked aggressively into Natasha's mouth. Many hands gripped Natasha's upper arms and wrists, pinning them to her sides. So fierce was the onslaught that Natasha froze, bodily and mentally. All she could think was that Chloe's breath was a sickly cocktail of stale alcohol, tobacco and dope.

Chloe's drink dropped to the floor and the glass shattered, but no one really noticed. A possessive hand cupped and mauled Natasha's breasts with little finesse, sadistically pinching her defenceless nipples. She tried to object to the violation, but the tongue simply wormed deeper, smothering her protestations into nothing more than muffled moans.

Then suddenly the kiss ended and Chloe stared venomously into her disbelieving eyes. 'You love it, don't you, miss prim and proper?' she hissed.

'Please,' Natasha whispered, squirming hopelessly against the arms that held her tightly from behind, 'why are you doing this to me?'

'Fuck why I'm doing this to you,' Chloe sniggered vehemently. 'If you won't take your clothes off when I ask nicely, we'll move on to the really good bit... on your knees.'

'No...' Natasha protested, immediately realising the girl's intentions. She tried to squirm free with desperate vigour, but the gang held her easily and the pressure on her shoulders and arms increased, forcing her down.

'Oh, fuck,' Chloe giggled, blinking blearily, the drink and dope making her sway on her feet. 'I forgot I was wearing these fucking silly trousers. I'm going to have to take the fuckers off before little miss goody-goody can do me properly with that wicked little tongue of hers.'

'No, please...' Natasha whimpered as she was forced down onto her knees and a fist grabbed her hair and pulled her head back, so she was staring at the red PVC crotch swaying inches before her face.

Chloe cupped Natasha's chin, holding her steady as she undid the button at the tight waist of her trousers and then fumbled for the zipper. 'Oh, don't be like that,' she cooed in mock disappointment. 'Just do as I tell you, like a good girl.'

The music came to an end and a tense silence fell over the room and across the group. Natasha held her breath, and could focus on nothing but the sight and sound of the zip, as Chloe tugged and it started to lower right before her horrified eyes...

And then the transfixed group jumped with a collective shriek as a stern voice thwarted the hateful ambush.

'Would someone please tell me what's going on in here?!' boomed Evelyn Marnie.

The next morning Natasha slept late. When she eventually got up it was close to midday, and with an aching head – the result of excessive alcohol the night before – she ventured down to the kitchen for a coffee.

To her horror Jean was there. But this was a very different figure from the one at the failed initiation ceremony. She was pale, her hair lay untidily around her shoulders, and she was dressed in shapeless dungarees. Two cigarette butts lay in a saucer – a clear breach of the house rules. She avoided eye contact with Natasha and muttered that the kettle had just boiled.

'Miss Marnie says I'm to apologise to you reservedly,' she eventually mumbled when Natasha sat opposite her at the large pine table, a steaming mug of coffee cupped in her hands.

'I think she probably said unreservedly, but I'll take it in the spirit you intended,' Natasha said benevolently. 'Why did you behave so badly towards me, Jean? I'd done nothing to you.'

'Chloe leads us on,' Jean said. 'You know, we're easily led. That's what Miss Marnie tells us, anyway.'

'Maybe she's got a point.'

'And she certainly knows how to make it.' The girl grimaced as she shifted on her chair.

Natasha was a little puzzled. 'What do you mean?'

she asked.

'Ask Chloe when she gets out.'

'Gets out? From where?'

'From Miss Marnie's room.'

Natasha took a careful sip of the hot coffee and pondered Jean's words for a while. 'What's she doing in Miss Marnie's room?' she eventually asked.

'You should be asking what she's having done to her,' Jean said with feeling.

Natasha could get no sense out of Jean, but somehow she had to get to the bottom of what she was being told. So, feeling revived by the hot coffee, she left the kitchen and climbed the backstairs to the attic level, and tiptoed along the passage to Evelyn's room. Even as she approached she could hear from behind the closed door soft noises, like the whimpering of someone or something in pain.

Cautiously she approached the two steps leading up to the door. There was a murmur that she recognised as Evelyn's voice. It was a question, repeated, more loudly this time, but Natasha could not make out what it was. Then there was a harsh and abrupt retort followed by a gasp.

Carefully kneeling on the top step she could put an eye to the large keyhole, and was immediately able to take in most of what was happening in the tiny attic room.

She saw Evelyn's back. She wore a dark shirt, and amazingly, leather jeans that gleamed moodily in the afternoon sun that penetrated into the room through the dormer window. They were quite at odds to her usual formal dress code.

As she moved to one side Natasha could see Chloe standing in the sentry box aperture created by the dormer. She was standing sideways on to the window, her profile silhouetted by the sunlight. Over the end of Evelyn's bed a white garment was draped. Chloe was wearing jeans, but her breasts were bare, and she stood with both hands linked on top of her cropped head.

Evelyn moved and once again obscured the view. The question was repeated. She was carrying a riding crop. It was raised with amazing speed and cut down viciously, making even Natasha flinch. She could only guess where the girl was being struck, but her whimpering indicated the extent of her pain.

Natasha realised the punishment must be on account of what had happened to her in the dance room. This was terrible. She immediately felt responsible that Chloe was being treated so severely.

Natasha watched as Evelyn stood back and surveyed her victim. The woman moved with a poise and confidence that announced her total control over the proceedings.

And what a pitiful contrast Chloe made. Her chin was held high, but she was continually glancing sideways, clearly dreading what was to follow. As Natasha watched, unable to think what to do, Evelyn brought the tip of the crop up to eye level, and with two quick flicks of the wrist she assaulted both Chloe's poor breasts. Chloe cried out, her feeble utterance coming from the back of her throat; a groan of resignation, with a hint of satisfaction. Her arms came down and she cradled her breasts to defend them from further attacks.

But Evelyn cast the crop onto the bed and approached the girl menacingly. Chloe backed away, but within a tiny stride she was pinned against the windowsill as Evelyn grabbed one of her wrists and twisted it behind her back. Natasha wondered why Chloe didn't put up more of a struggle.

Evelyn turned and pushed her prey against the bed. Chloe stumbled and fell onto it with a cry. Evelyn swung one black leather-clad knee across her stomach and sat astride the girl as she lay on her back.

Again there were repeated questions. Clearly the replies were inadequate, because Evelyn brought out of her shirt pocket two identical disks of metal.

She held one up to demonstrate. Natasha could see that, as she squeezed it, a set of tiny jaws opened and then closed again as she relaxed her grip. Natasha saw her reach down and, with evident relish, take a nipple between thumb and finger and applied one of the spiteful clamps. Chloe's head rolled tormentedly from side to side, but she made no sound.

Evelyn applied the second clamp, and Natasha thought she caught a glimpse of a smile on the face of the woman who was supposed to be looking after the welfare of the girls in her charge.

Then Evelyn produced a fine silver chain, which she dangled provocatively over Chloe's face. In a second she had each end hooked to the clamps and was now able to manipulate Chloe as and how she wanted. She pulled at first one breast and then the other, making them rise to a sharp peak, and then letting them subside just as suddenly. Poor Chloe couldn't get used to the way her breasts were being treated, but every time she attempted to get free Evelyn tugged viciously on the chain.

Chloe was now squealing with the discomfort, her arms folded over her face. Natasha couldn't watch any more, so she got off her knees and flung the door open, to be greeted by a moment of astonished silence.

Evelyn was clearly taken aback, but then she

regained her poise as she slid off the bed.

'Natasha, this is certainly a surprise,' she said, her tone syrupy. 'Were you never taught that it's polite to knock before entering a room?'

Natasha couldn't believe the woman's bullish attitude. 'Evelyn, what are you doing to Chloe?' she blurted.

Evelyn smiled down at Chloe, who was raising herself to kneel beside her, and stroked her hair. 'To answer your rather impertinent question,' she said, 'I was punishing Chloe for her bad behaviour toward you last night.'

The victim in question moulded herself against Evelyn's leather-clad thigh, like a cat wanting a saucer of milk. Natasha could see the marks of the crop sharply defined in angry read weals on her breasts. 'Chloe, are you all right?' she asked. 'I'm sorry you've had to go through this. Believe me, if Evelyn had asked me first I would not have sanctioned such barbaric punishment.'

'Thanks for nothing, new girl,' Chloe purred, putting an arm around Evelyn's waist.

'B-but,' Natasha stammered. 'I don't understand... I don't understand at all.'

'Well perhaps I can explain, Natasha,' said Evelyn, as though explaining something to a simpleton. 'Chloe is my creature. She does exactly as I say. She knows that if she transgresses she will be punished. Just recently she has been transgressing rather a lot, I'm afraid. Turn around and show Natasha, Chloe.'

Chloe swivelled round. Against the pale skin of her buttocks the criss-crosses of the lash marks were shockingly defined. She looked over her shoulder and grinned broadly.

Natasha felt sick. 'You mean, she enjoys the

vicious treatment you dish out?' she said incredulously.

'Like I said, she is my creature,' Evelyn confirmed. 'I had to break her in just like the others. You'd be surprised how easily the boundaries between pleasure and pain can be obscured. The girls who come here must learn to control their mind and body and ignore discomfort. I am only helping them in that process. Perhaps I could help you too, Natasha. Come, shut the door, and we can start forthwith.'

Natasha hesitated, then spun round and scurried back down the stairs to her room, the mocking laughter of the girl and her tormentor in cruel pursuit.

Chapter 4

Natasha did not mention the incident to Saffron when she returned after the weekend. Why not, she wondered? Partly it was embarrassment. But there was a feeling of unease that she couldn't dispel about how far Evelyn's influence spread through the Academy. For all Natasha knew, Saffron might also be involved. So she would proceed with caution until she knew how things stood.

In the meantime she had to work on getting her book together. For any serious newcomer to the world of modelling she knew a portfolio of stunning photos was essential. It had to show off one's best physical features and, if possible, cuttings of shows and promotions. Natasha was a little apprehensive about her first shoot; a free session with a photographer named Monty had been arranged.

They had to get as many poses as possible in an hour or so. She and Astrid would then look at all the contact prints and select the ones to print up for her book. Only then could Astrid start approaching the fashion and PR clients who were looking for fresh faces.

Wardour Photography was situated in a pleasant row of old brick houses that had mainly been converted into studios and offices. She was welcomed by Fiona – a strange combination of red dreadlocks and biker leathers – who announced that she doubled as assistant and receptionist. She took Natasha through to the back and showed her the changing area.

Natasha had brought along three changes; a simple black dress, a mini and matching jacket she'd designed herself, and a more daring boob tube and an embroidered jeans combo. She also had in her bag a thong bikini. She wasn't sure about this, but it was just in case she felt relaxed enough to model it.

She was not reassured by the changing area which was basically a shower curtain affair in one corner of the studio, a full-length mirror, some pegs on the wall and a small shelf upon which was an iron. There wasn't enough room to swing a cat, but checking the curtain was pulled to the wall, she began to undress.

The next minute the curtain swished aside and Fiona popped her head inside, a big grin on her freckled face.

'Hi, how are you getting on?' she beamed. 'Can I help zip you up?'

'Oh, er, thanks,' said Natasha, feeling a little flustered by the girl's forthright approach. 'By the way,' she ventured, 'is there a make-up girl here?'

'Afraid not. This is a wee favour for the Academy, you understand. Anyway, don't worry, if you start to glisten I'll have the powder puff ready.'

'Glisten?'

'Yeah, under the lights. Is this your very first time?'

Natasha nodded.

'Oh, well don't worry, your Auntie Fiona will show you the ropes.'

Natasha knew she was blushing as she hastily adjusted the mini. This was just the sort of thing she had hoped to avoid. Why couldn't Fiona go away, instead of standing there, leaning against the wall and being unnecessarily friendly?

'Nice jacket,' Fiona said approvingly. 'And you've a good figure. Are you going to be doing glamour too?'

'You mean, like stripping down to my underwear? Well, I, um, brought along a bikini... just in case—'

'That's terrific,' Fiona enthused. 'Monty's always keen to get a few tit shots. I can tell you they won't do your book any harm. These days you need to be able to display your chest on the catwalk without feeling inhibited.'

'Well, I just don't know...' it was all moving a bit too fast for Natasha's liking. 'I'll wait and see how confident I feel later on in the session.'

After twenty minutes or so Natasha was beginning to feel a little more relaxed. Against her better judgement she'd accepted the couple of premium lagers that were offered to her whilst changing, and the results, on an almost empty stomach, were virtually immediate. She felt a little light-headed, reclining on cushions in the calf-length black dress, Monty encouraging her to lie back and show more cleavage and thigh.

The lights were hot. She took another drink of lager in the changing room as she slipped quickly into the embellished flower-power jeans and the tube top.

'Well, that's something a bit special,' Monty complimented her, as he set up the tripod with a new camera. 'Now, my dear, how revealing do you want this set to be?'

'I – I don't know, really,' Natasha admitted. 'What do you advise?' She was beginning to feel quite safe posing in front of Monty. His bland looks and receding hairline made him seem pretty harmless. But it wasn't Monty who answered her question.

'Why don't you pull down the top a little so the camera gets more of your breasts and cleavage?' Fiona suggested. 'What do you say to that?'

It seemed fair enough, so Natasha began to ease it down with her thumbs. Before she knew it she had exposed one nipple. It was a little engorged, and she felt a pleasant tingling sensation as it sprang free of the clingy fabric. Then the other one was revealed, and she suddenly found it difficult to control her breathing. Her mouth was dry, and she couldn't think of anything to say.

'You really are lovely, Natasha,' Fiona oozed, moving close and taking her by the shoulders. She led her to a high bar stool and placed her in a provocative pose, stood out of shot to one side, and seemed to be giving signs to Monty on how to frame his shots. It was a strange situation, but Natasha was feeling too relaxed to care.

She eased the top edge of her top down even further. Now both her breasts were fully exposed, and as if in a dream she put her hands under them to emphasise their fullness. The tips began to stiffen even more, responsive to the sensation.

Her uncertainty evaporated, and soon the tight top was off entirely and she was perched jauntily on the stool with both hands around one knee. Then she felt

Fiona's warm hands slip under her arms and cradle her breasts. She looked around and was confronted by that reassuringly ever-present grin.

'How are you taking to your first shoot, Natasha?' the woman asked huskily.

Natasha tried to gather her thoughts, her mind in a whirl of conflicting responses. 'I... well, it's no worse than I'd feared,' she whispered, all thoughts of Monty and the watching camera forgotten.

Fiona was holding one of her nipples and rolling it gently between thumb and forefinger while whispering encouragement in her ear. The dark teats stood out hard and proud. Contentedly, Natasha lay her head back against Fiona's shoulder, sighed, and closed her eyes. She felt her long hair being gently stroked, and loved it. It reminded her of bedtime when she was small, her mother crooning a Lithuanian lullaby.

'So, are we ready?' Monty's voice was more urgent than before.

'Okay, Natasha, let's do some glamour,' Fiona urged softly, and her hands glided down to the waistband of Natasha's jeans. 'Let's have these off, shall we?'

The button flies were easily popped undone, and then Fiona moved round, careful not to alarm her new plaything, and crouched to ease off her ankle boots. Then, from her crouched position, she helped Natasha ease her bottom off the stool and stand, a little unsteadily, then pulled the soft jeans over her hips and down her smooth bare legs. A little tugging and they were free of Natasha's ankles and feet, and Fiona draped the crumpled denim over one arm.

Monty moved closer, his auto-wind whirring continuously. The effects of the drink seemed to increase, and Natasha felt more and more relaxed, instinctively easing from one sexy pose to another. Monty seemed to like what she was doing, for he fired out directions and encouragement.

Fiona intervened again, moving her from the stool and replacing it with a plastic chair. Natasha sat on it with her legs pulled under her and her head thrown back.

'That's really good, Natasha,' Fiona cooed, with Monty shooting rapidly. 'Now let's see you be a bit more provocative. Show how much of a real woman you are.'

Natasha wasn't sure, but again followed her instincts. She stood up, and with her hands on the back of the chair, arched her back and ground her bottom at the camera, her soft buttocks barely concealed by the taut crisp cotton of her panties.

'That's really sexy,' Fiona enthused. 'Give it more if you can.' She was close again, and Natasha felt her take the waistband and pull the skimpy cotton down just over the curve of her rump. Natasha shivered excitedly, and could feel a pooling of moist heat between her legs.

'That wasn't so bad, now was it?' Fiona said softly. 'You're a natural, Natasha,' and she put an arm around her shoulder. She had taken off her leather jacket and both it and Natasha's jeans lay over the back of a chair, well out of reach.

Behind her Natasha heard a rustling. She turned round in time to see the white backer being rolled up like a giant window blind. Behind it, to her great surprise, was a fairly basic set; an old-fashioned kitchen range and a bare pine table, and a large camera already set up on a tripod.

'What's all this for?' she asked, still feeling nice and calm. 'What's going on, Fiona?'

'Natasha, honey, do you really not know what

we're doing next? The Academy gets these sessions for free. But the deal is we can only give you the prints if you agree to do a special.'

Natasha's brow furrowed as she tried to work out what she was being told. 'Special?' she said. 'What sort of special?'

'It's just a little spanking session, with me,' Fiona explained in a sultry tone. 'Monty will take a few snaps, and we'll keep your face well hidden if you want. I won't do it too hard, I promise.'

Fiona had a hand on Natasha's bottom, and was steering her towards the table. She spoke softly and hypnotically. Natasha knew there was something wrong with this turn of events, but somehow she couldn't work out a way of getting out of it, and didn't know whether she wanted to.

However, things happened rather more quickly than Natasha had imagined they would. Fiona bent her forward across the table and told her to grip the far edge. She did, as if in a dream. It was a scenario she had experienced before, with that familiar feeling of inevitability.

She jerked on the tabletop as she heard a loud smack and felt the harsh strike on her right buttock. Suddenly feeling somewhat uneasy with the situation she'd fallen into, she struggled to rise from her position across the table, but Fiona's hand was quickly between her shoulders to hold her firmly in place.

Then the blows came with the regularity of a metronome. Fiona was obviously an experienced spanker, striking with formidable power and accuracy, and had Natasha's cotton panties still been nestled snugly over her buttocks, they would have provided scant protection.

Monty hovered in the background, clicking away,

concentrating on the alluring view.

After a short while Natasha, deep down, started to warm to the treatment she was receiving, and then the spanking stopped, and delicate fingers slipped between her legs and found her shameful wetness. Fiona's other hand stroked down Natasha's spine, causing her to sigh and arch her back, and then it was massaging her buttocks, fingertips delving into the deep shadowy valley that separated the lush globes of punished flesh.

Natasha stiffened a little with conflicting emotions. She didn't really want to reveal to Fiona, Monty, or the camera the state of her arousal, but on the other hand, she was just about beyond caring, such was the skill of Fiona's touch.

'Are they sore, Natasha?' Fiona whispered, the camera still working, almost forgotten by the girl spread across the table, such was the pleasure she was savouring. 'Your sweet buttocks... are they sore?'

Natasha sighed again and nodded, her eyes closed as she drifted on a cloud of delight.

And then the hands and fingers were gone, and for some reason Fiona had drawn a sudden and, as far as Natasha was concerned, untimely halt to the proceedings.

'There,' she said, slightly breathlessly, confirming Natasha's fears, 'I think that will do for now.'

Natasha had known a lovely orgasm was building, but the drink had numbed any sense of embarrassment. Now though, spread wantonly over the table with Fiona and Monty once again bustling busily around the studio, shame and regret swept over her. She sensed that for some unknown reason they were playing a cruel game with her, and she cringed as she pushed herself upright and pulled her panties up, the discomfort in her spanked buttocks as the soft material snugly encased them only matched by the discomfort induced by her shamefully lewd performance.

'Fiona? Monty?' she eventually spoke up. 'What's been going on here?'

'Oh, nothing,' Fiona answered evasively. 'It's just a little arrangement we have.'

'Arrangement?' Natasha didn't like what she was hearing. 'What sort of an arrangement.'

'It's really nothing for you to worry your pretty little head about,' said Fiona, smiling patronisingly, while Monty avoided eye contact with Natasha and busied himself with moving the odd light or tripod.

Later that week the contacts did at least arrive, and thankfully they stopped just at the point where Natasha's top had come off. Still feeling ashamed at herself and angry at Fiona and Monty for taking advantage, she decided to say nothing about the episode to Astrid, and with the woman's help she selected around a dozen images for her book and tried to forget what had happened, putting it down to experience.

'Now, I can talk to some of the bookers,' said Astrid. 'There are some autumn collections coming up, but in the meantime I'll need to get back some of the money I've spent on you. You're my investment. How do you feel about some promotion work?'

'I'm happy if you're happy,' said Natasha. 'But I don't want to get involved with anything dodgy.'

Astrid smiled knowingly. 'You've so much more savvy than so many of the others, Natasha,' she said. 'I'm going to call you my wise little owl.'

Laughing, she pulled Natasha towards her and gave her a hug. Astrid seemed only to have her welfare at heart and she had been more than generous to her. Was it possible she didn't know what was going on with Fiona and Monty?

There was a knock on the door and Evelyn came into the office.

'Ah Evelyn,' Astrid welcomed her, 'we've just finished looking through the results of Natasha's first photo session. I think she's very pleased with them. I am, and I'm certainly hopeful that she'll land some nice bookings for us very soon.'

Natasha left the two women to discuss Academy business and went to a session of nutrition revision in the quiet room. She didn't know what to think of Evelyn. She was a control freak without a doubt, and seemed to enjoy humiliating the girls. But on the other hand maybe the discipline thing, although unduly harsh, was a sign of her own insecurity.

She had almost fallen asleep over her revision when Jean thrust a piece of paper on the table in front of her. She recognised handwriting as Evelyn's:

I need to discuss certain disciplinary matters with you. Report to the office at 7 o'clock this evening, prompt.

'Try to keep on the right side of her, Natasha,' Saffron advised ominously, when Natasha later showed her the note and asked what she thought of it. 'It will make life here much easier for all of us.' But she would say no more.

And so, it was with a sense of foreboding and bewilderment that Natasha approached the door of Evelyn's office. But the stern command to enter, following her timid knock, came from behind Astrid's office door, which was a little further down the corridor and slightly ajar. It opened with a portentous creak as she pushed against it and entered, and then reluctantly closed it behind her with a solid finality. Evelyn sat at Astrid's imposing desk.

'Sit down, Natasha,' she said. 'I want us to have a little chat.'

'I – I got your note,' Natasha said, a little stupidly she realised, otherwise why else would she be there? 'What do you want to see me about?'

'I just want to make one or two things clear in case there's any doubt in your mind,' the woman said.

Natasha sat on the rigid straight-backed chair placed before Astrid's antique kneehole desk. They faced each other across the leather-topped expanse. Evelyn, dressed in dark grey, sat with her hands clasped in front of her on the desktop.

'Are you enjoying your stay at the Academy, Natasha?' she asked.

'I am... thank you.'

'Even after that unfortunate incident during your first week.'

'The initiation, you mean?' Natasha started to relax a little, feeling that perhaps she wasn't in for a hard time, after all. 'Oh, I've put that behind me. But I was rather upset with what you and Chloe were up to afterwards.'

'Ah yes, Chloe.' Evelyn smiled enigmatically. 'It was partly about Chloe that I wanted to speak to you, my dear.'

The sweet tones reminded Natasha of that first day when she was invited up to the woman's room. This time she would try and resist the charm offensive.

'Natasha, my dear, I don't think you quite understand your situation here. You seem to think that because you are a little older than the other girls you can do as you please.'

'But that's not so, I—'

'For example,' Evelyn went on, ignoring the interruption, 'you dare to question my behaviour with Chloe. It is entirely my decision as to how infringements such as those perpetrated by her on Saturday evening are to be handled. And you must accept this, if you are to continue here at the Academy.'

'And does Astrid know just how you handle these infringements?' Natasha challenged, gradually feeling less intimidated by the austere woman.

'I keep her informed sufficiently, I think. Why do you ask? I hope you're not thinking of going behind my back. I like to develop close relationships with some of the girls purely for teaching purposes. I would certainly be very upset if I thought you were misrepresenting my activities to Astrid. So were you thinking of going behind my back?'

'No, I wasn't,' said Natasha. 'But I'm unhappy about the strict way you handle some of them.'

'Are you calling me a tyrant?' Evelyn smiled tightly, peering over her wire-framed glasses at her. It irritated Natasha that the older woman thought she could intimidate her so simply.

'Maybe not, Evelyn, but if I see anything that I judge harmful then I would feel—'

'Feel what, exactly?'

'I would feel unhappy to let it go unreported. I know you mean well, Evelyn, but sometimes I think your influence on the more impressionable girls may be, well, unhealthy.'

'My God, Natasha, who on earth do you think you are? What business is it of yours how I do or do not control the girls? I warn you here and now that if you go behind my back you will pay for it most severely.'

'You've got no hold over me, Evelyn,' Natasha said defiantly. 'I'm not interested in becoming one of your favourites, so I won't succumb to your bullying tactics.'

Evelyn smiled confidently, and suddenly the tension eased. 'I believe you were at Wardour Photography yesterday,' she said.

'Um, I was, yes,' Natasha said, suddenly thrown off balance by Evelyn's apparent change of mood. 'What of it?'

'Fiona happens to be a very good friend of mine. Oh, didn't she tell you?' The woman was mocking Natasha. 'She and I share many things.'

Natasha couldn't believe her ears. 'Y-you mean, you know about the... the photographs?' she stammered. 'You've seen them, haven't you?'

Evelyn shook her head. 'Not yet. But I shall, Natasha. And believe me, I'm greatly looking forward to it. She says you took to being spanked with real enthusiasm, but she thought your attitude could improve somewhat.'

'So what exactly are you saying?' Natasha asked cautiously.

'What I'm saying is, my dear, quite simply, that unless you show the respect due to me those extra photos will also somehow get to Astrid.'

'So she knows nothing about the sordid little deal you've got going there?'

'Blissfully ignorant, my dear,' Evelyn said, with a glee that seemed at odds with her austere persona. 'And for obvious reasons that's just the way I want it to stay.'

'You mean, it's just an arrangement between you and that two-faced Fiona?'

Evelyn didn't reply. Her contented expression said

it all. She sat back and her swivel chair creaked quietly as she turned to the side and stretched out her legs.

'Now, to show me that your attitude has changed,' she said smugly, 'why don't you come round here and take off these shoes for me? It's been a long day, and my feet ache.'

Natasha swallowed her surprise and indignation of the suggestion. She wasn't the woman's skivvy, but if she was to get the better of her she must use her head. She stood with as much outward pride as she could muster, walked around the desk with her chin high, and then knelt at the woman's feet.

'On you go, my dear,' the woman directed, staring down at the kneeling girl.

Natasha gripped the back of one shoe, and as she eased it off Evelyn lifted her knee slightly, causing her skirt to ride up her thighs. Was this some sort of invitation? Natasha tried not to look, but beneath the skirt the shadowy triangle of pale material covering the woman's sex drew her eye.

Evelyn sighed with contentment as first one shoe, and then the other one came off.

'Now, you may smell it,' she said, nodding at the shoe in Natasha's hands, taking her completely by surprise with such a suggestion. 'All my girls agree to. As a token of their loyalty, you understand.'

Natasha shook her head in bewilderment. 'No... I mean, do I really have to?'

Evelyn nodded and smiled confidently. 'You most certainly do, if you wish to stay on my good side.'

'Let me unlace the other one first.'

It was all so demeaning, but knowing she had little choice but to comply, Natasha slowly lifted the shoe to her face and sniffed, and to her surprise, the odour was not unpleasant, the warm leather providing the dominant bittersweet scents. She looked up again at Evelyn, who was still watching her like a cat.

'There, Natasha,' the woman mused contentedly. 'Perhaps you have the makings of a fetishist in you after all. And don't look so sulky, it was supposed to be a compliment,' she tutted. 'You see, we get on quite well together, when you relax.'

She leant forward on her chair, took the shoe from Natasha's hands, placed it on the floor with its partner, and then raised her fingertips to Natasha's chin, lifting it to stare deeply into Natasha's wide eyes. Natasha new she was breathing rapidly, and tried to calm herself as Evelyn leant even closer and brushed a cheek with her lips.

Then Evelyn, still smiling enigmatically, stood and moved away, and Natasha heard the key turn in the lock. Evelyn took off her jacket and placed it, neatly folded, on the desk, and then sat again on her chair, opening her thighs slightly and holding Natasha between her legs. 'Now, my dear,' she said huskily, 'you will do something for me. Do you understand?'

'I...' Natasha wanted to object, but she paused, realised the futility of refusing the woman anything, and nodded meekly.

'Good girl,' the woman said. 'It will demonstrate that you are now fully committed to accepting my authority here.'

Natasha felt trapped, locked in the claustrophobic office with such a domineering female. 'Evelyn, I'm not a lesbian, okay?' she said defensively.

The woman sat tall, towering possessively over the kneeling girl. 'Of course, my dear, if you say so,' she purred.

'So – so what is it you want from me?' stammered Natasha.

The eyes of the predator woman glinted behind her glasses as she clearly sensed her goal was within touching distance. 'Just a little kiss, my dear. Will you do that for me?'

Natasha hesitated, looking up at the woman, and then nodded.

Evelyn smiled again, and stroked Natasha's hair. 'Good girl,' she purred again. 'I knew you wouldn't disappoint me.' And then, to Natasha's horror and disbelief, the woman held the hem of her skirt with her free hand, and began to ease it up her thighs, lifting her bottom slightly from the chair to ease its tantalising passage.

Natasha felt sick as she realised, with increasing certainty, what kind of kiss it was to be. In a daze and finding herself unable to resist, she allowed Evelyn to put a hand to the back of her head and pull her slowly down and forward, closer between her thighs. Natasha closed her eyes and prepared for the inevitable. Stockings and then flesh touched her cheeks. Evelyn, growing increasingly eager, pulled aside the damp crotch of her panties. Natasha felt she was being manipulated like a puppet, and she was no match for Evelyn's strength or authority. Black curls brushed her lips, springy and dense.

She instinctively pursed her lips to make the lightest of contacts, but still all control was out of her hands. Evelyn pressed roughly on the back of her head to ensure a firm contact, grinding her hips on the chair and groaning a deep, guttural groan. She was clearly deriving the utmost pleasure from taking advantage of such a gorgeous girl as Natasha. She looked down dreamily, encouraging her with languid smiles and a pout of her lips. 'That's lovely, my dear,' she cooed, pressing her hips forward even more urgently. 'You're doing very well.'

Natasha was unable to move or pull away, pinned as she was between the woman's legs, with a possessive hand guiding her head. Then the grip in her hair increased, almost painfully, and Evelyn made sure her prey was glued to the spot from which her mounting ecstasy issued. She would not release her until she was spent.

Natasha was enveloped by the intimate odours of the woman's sex, trapped in her springy bush. Her lips and chin were smeared with glistening fluid as Evelyn groaned, rocking on the chair in wild abandon, her head thrown back. Then, with a final shudder and a keening cry she climaxed, her legs clamped around Natasha, and then she slumped, drained and replete on the chair, her eyes closed and her breasts rising and falling deeply as her breathing slowed.

In tears, Natasha got to her feet and ran straight to the door, still tasting the musky essence of Evelyn's quim. She turned the key and turned to face her oppressor.

'You're nothing but a vicious bully, Evelyn, and I shall never ever respect your authority,' she sobbed. 'You don't deserve it.'

She flung the door open and scurried out of the office, and once again she heard the harsh peals of mocking laughter pursuing her as she fled.

Chapter 5

Natasha couldn't bear to stay for another week at the Academy. She just had to get away. Evelyn's poisonous influence was choking her. By coincidence, her mother had phoned from Edinburgh to ask if she were coming up for her exhibition opening that weekend. It was a great opportunity to get away, for a while, at least. Astrid confirmed that there were no definite bookings yet, but she had strong indications of some materialising. If anything urgent came up she had Natasha's mother's number in Scotland.

To feel this sense of release in returning to the home of her teenage years was strange. Edinburgh had once been a killjoy kind of place where traditionally lace curtains always twitched. Then once a year it was festival time and the streets were like perpetual Mardi Gras. Now, however, with the transfer of political power, the city had an almost manic buzz. It felt rather like hearing a maiden aunt was taking up bungee jumping.

As soon as Natasha stepped off the train and looked up to the Castle Rock she knew the festival was underway. There was a row of flagpoles with bright colours flying in the stiff breeze. Every night they had the military tattoo up there on the esplanade – a fantastic sight. And then there was the fireworks display with cascades of light down those black cliffs, which rose so dramatically from the Princes Street gardens.

The streets of the old town were crowded with noise and movement. Students usually dressed in costume pushed leaflets into the hands or pockets of passers-by. At the foot of The Mound on Princes Street a huge crowd watched a red-wigged clown apparently defy gravity by climbing up with legs spread between two massive stone columns. When he reached almost to the underside of the portico he stopped and began to juggle. There was a wild madness that had overrun the graceful city. Natasha breathed in its refreshing air gratefully.

Her mother lived in a large four-storey terraced house in the west end. It had been far too big for just the two of them. She would have moved out, were it not for the fact that as a painter she could store all her canvases and other creations. Hopefully not in every room, prayed Natasha, as she let herself in, discovered no one was around and went up to the first floor where a large room with a bow window overlooked the street.

With relief she saw that everything was exactly as she remembered it from a year before. How wonderful it was to have a room to herself again. And not just any room, but the one where she'd spent her girlhood, with all its souvenirs and familiar reminders.

She threw her holdall and rucksack on the floor, and impulsively, she picked up a flop-eared bunny to hold it to her face and breathe in its smell.

Then she heard the front door opening and closing and footsteps in the hall. It must be her mother. She opened the bedroom door and bounded down the stairs, and then stopped short with a gasp. Facing her, silhouetted in the light from the fan-shaped window over the door, was a powerfully built man in a dark suit.

'You must be Natasha,' he said bluntly. 'Your mother said I'm to look for you. She will return soon, she says. I'm Semyon Chavadze.'

He extended his hand and she descended the final steps to take it. The skin felt ice cold.

'Of course,' she said, feeling uneasy in the stranger's presence, 'my mother did say she'd let the upstairs flat for the festival, but I'd forgotten.'

'You're right,' he said. 'I am indeed that lodger.'

He smiled, but Natasha still found him intimidating with his darkly glinting eyes and the blue haze of his jowls and chin. She realised he was younger than she had first thought, and probably Russian, but right now she didn't really want to get into a long conversation; she was wanting to find out if any of her college chums were around. But she ought to be polite to her mother's paying guest.

'Oh, that's nice,' she said. 'So you're here just for the festival, Mr Chavadze?'

'Please, call me Semyon,' he said. 'Yes, I am impresario, you understand, for east European artists.'

'For the festival programme?'

'Yes, and also for the Fringe. Your mother also. You know she is to have an exhibition at the new festival centre?'

'Oh, thanks for reminding me.' Natasha smiled, but wondered how she could get away.

'And a reception too,' he added. 'She will be so pleased you are here in time.'

He gave an unctuous smile and spread his hands, almost as if he was going to embrace her.

'Do you know where my mother is?' she asked.

'She will be here soon. I think she has gone out for shopping. She wishes to cook you a meal of welcome.'

Natasha's heart sank. Although daring and creative, her mother's cooking was rarely successful when it came to making something that could safely be eaten. So Natasha decided to make her escape if she could before her mother arrived.

Excusing herself guiltily to the lodger, she made a couple of phone calls and discovered that Leon was still in town. Better than that, he was involved in staging a show for the festival fringe with some other members of the dramatic society, otherwise known as DramSoc. It was a case of all helpers welcome as the production opened the following night.

She agreed to meet up with Leon and the cast at the art college where a studio was being used for the dress rehearsal. It brought back fond memories as she walked in and was greeted by the familiar smells of paint and linseed. The place was packed with students, some in costume.

In the far corner she caught Leon's eye. He smiled and pointed up to the mezzanine balcony. There was no one else up there, but a few canvases were stacked up at the far end. She knelt down on the floor and peered over the edge. From here she had a better view of what was going on, since there was a large cast with a chorus. A piano was thumping out a melody and someone was singing loudly, if not very harmoniously.

However, the costumes of various trollops, fishwives and ne'er-do-wells were very impressive. She spotted one or two familiar faces busy pinning up skirts and fixing décolletages. For once fashion textile design was going to get top billing.

Natasha wondered if McGruer had given the show her blessing, and then she heard someone climbing the wooden stairs to join her. First she saw a shock of ginger hair and then a matching beard that was not immediately familiar.

'Hello, Natasha, Leon said you were coming,' said the man.

'Hello, it's Rory, isn't it?' she responded politely. 'For a moment I didn't recognise you with the beard. How long have you had it?'

'I grew it during last summer vac,' Rory told her. 'Took a long time, so I wanted to be seen with it fully formed. Thank goodness it matches.' He gave the shy grin that Natasha remembered from her student days.

'Are you still doing graphic design?' she asked. 'I remember you dragged me out a couple of times to those weird black and white French films.'

Rory grinned, and suddenly Natasha realised faces were turned in their direction. They must have been talking louder than she had realised. The rehearsal was being distracted, so Rory squatted down beside her and they conversed in whispers.

'So, Natasha,' he said, 'why have you come back to Edinburgh?'

'It's just for a break from London really. I'm at a modelling school and things were getting a bit... well, heavy. I'm staying at my mum's for a few days. So why are you here?'

He turned and looked at her. They were by necessity very close to each other, conducting their conversation in whispers, and Natasha suddenly realised this was the first man she had really talked to in the last few weeks since leaving Jim.

'I came to meet you, of course,' he said. 'And then again, I am supposed to be producing the programme for The Resurrection Men.'

'The what men?'

'Burke and Hare, the murderous pair who supplied bodies for the early surgeons to experiment with,' Rory explained. 'They were known as resurrection men because they raised bodies from the grave. That was before they turned to supplying fresh cadavers themselves. I'm surprised a well-brought up Edinburgh lass like you needs to be told this by an uncouth Glaswegian.'

She felt herself blush. Rory was much more assured than she remembered him being a year before. It would be nice to get to know him again.

Just then a girl in pigtails Natasha recognised

popped her head up and approached them both with a slightly timid smile.

'Hi, you're Natasha, aren't you?' she asked. 'You used to be in Fabric and Fashion didn't you?'

'Hi, yes, and you're Jeanette,' Natasha said. 'I remember you design costumes for DramSoc. Does Leon want us to leave because we're causing a disturbance?'

'Oh no, not at all,' said the girl. 'Actually, he sort of thought you might be willing to help us with costumes. We're a bit short-handed, you see.'

'Of course I will,' Natasha said cheerily, only too glad to be of some help. 'I'll come right down.'

She and Rory said goodbye, but not before he had asked if she knew about the opening night party.

Natasha got home well before dinnertime, but that wasn't hard since her mother always ate late, particularly in the summer when she wanted to take advantage of the evening light which streamed in through the window of a back room she used as her studio.

She did not look well, Natasha thought. Even with her dark complexion the bags under her eyes were noticeable. Natasha guessed that the strain of having to prepare for her own show was beginning to tell.

'Let me cook, mum,' Natasha offered. 'You catch the last of the light. I'll bring it through when it's ready. My cooking's improved, thanks to Jim. You'll see.'

She was able to throw together a cold couscous of steamed vegetables, mint leaves and some chicken wings she found in the freezer. It was all done in about half an hour, one of Kiki's favourite dishes. She must remember to phone to see if her friend could make it up for the weekend. Kiki had previously seen her mother's paintings and seemed to genuinely admire them, so she would appreciate an invitation to the opening party.

They ate the couscous on their knees in the studio as the rosy light faded from the room. All around them were canvases, most of them abstracts with a hint of mountainous landscape or a loch. Natasha was none too sure which were finished, so she just picked out one or two she liked. In fact, her mother's training was as a portrait painter and she still had the knack of getting an immediate likeness, whether of human or animal. Either way, she could have made a very reasonable income from her art.

But she was bored by doing what she called society art and had turned to abstracts, which very rarely sold. Her parents had fled Lithuania during the German occupation and moved to Scotland during the last war. She had married late and Natasha was their only child. Natasha's father, an architect, died while still only in his fifties, so as a child she had been much in the company of her grandmother while her mother worked with increasing frustration at the portraits.

Money had always been tight, especially as the big house needed more and more maintenance work. Natasha wondered how much longer her mother could go on living there. They talked about the money situation cursorily; her mother, as usual, just hoped that something would turn up. But she had recently dipped into savings to pay for repairs to the roof. Natasha knew her father had intended some of the money to go towards her education, but she hadn't the heart to raise this with her mother.

Before going to bed she called Kiki who had started a course in computer art and was tied up during most of the week. She said she would try and get up to Edinburgh for a long weekend, and they could then perhaps return south together.

The next day was spent working on final adjustments to the costumes for The Resurrection Men. They were at last on stage in an old lodging house that had been ingeniously converted to a Fringe venue. The room seated about one hundred, with the acting area going right up to the first row of seats, the actors almost in the laps of the audience. Was it all going to work? Tonight was the first night!

It was exhausting work with pinning and sewing needed for just about everyone keeping her and Jeanette busy all morning before the final run-through with lighting cues. But there was a great atmosphere, and Leon, who was playing Dr Knox's servant as well as directing, dished out encouragement to everyone. The first night party preparations were in full swing as well. Everyone was contributing something and it was to take place in Leon's flat, which was nearby.

Natasha returned home in the afternoon, and was met once again by Semyon in the hallway.

'Ah, Miss Natasha, I had hoped to find you,' he said. 'Your mother was still asleep this morning when the telephone sounded. I did not want her to be disturbed so I answered. You understand?'

'Yes, perfectly,' she assured him. 'Who was it?'

Once again she felt herself being fixed by the surly gaze that so intimidated her.

'It was a friend of yours, a Miss Kiki. She said that she was planning to arrive for the reception on Friday. This is good news, yes?'

Natasha beamed at the news. 'Very much. Kiki is a good friend.'

'She sounded very happy on the phone – very

friendly. Is she the same age as you?'

Natasha thought this was a strange question, but said, 'About the same. She's very artistic. In fact, she studied painting here in Edinburgh. She was very keen on the early twentieth century Russian painters. The Modernists, I think they're called.'

'Indeed they are,' he confirmed, nodding sagely. 'I have seen many of them in St Petersburg where I used to live.'

'You don't live there any more then?'

'No, London is my home at the moment.'

'Oh, really. Do you know many other Russians there?'

'Plenty,' he confirmed, 'but you must understand I am not Russian but Georgian, Miss Natasha.'

'I'm sorry,' she said. 'I should have realised from your name. Calling you a Russian is a bit like someone telling me I'm English.'

For the first time Natasha saw his expression soften into a smile, and for a fleeting moment she could see the man of sentiment that lay underneath.

The Resurrection Men was a great success. They had managed almost a full house, thanks to friends and supporters at the college. A good notice in The Scotsman and they would be sure at least of being able to pay their running costs.

In great good spirits, and many of the cast still in low-life costumes, they trooped through the Grassmarket to Leon's flat. Natasha had changed out of her jeans into a strapless blue print dress.

It was a mild evening, so untypical of the rocky city, and they could hear the skirl of pipes from the castle ramparts above them. It had been a wonderful evening, but for Natasha, something was lacking.

She had been busy backstage for the first half, but

at the interval she looked for Rory in the audience. She'd quite taken to him, and was disappointed when there was no sign of him being there – then or since.

'Onward and upward,' Leon shouted as they turned into a common entrance that serviced the tenement block.

And he wasn't joking. The stone stairs seemed unending, but at last they reached the top landing with three front doors off it. Would Rory be able to find his way there, she wondered, as Leon flung open the middle one?

She started to chat with one of the chorus of fishwives who had taken a solo in the first act. In the second she had her throat cut by Burke. She was in her final year and knew Rory, and thought he probably wouldn't come. He wasn't a very sociable type, in her opinion.

But Rory did show eventually, at around midnight. He explained that he'd just missed them at the theatre and didn't have Leon's address. A drunk he talked to in desperation confirmed seeing a troop of strangely attired revellers heading in this direction but couldn't confirm which entrance they had turned into.

There were five or six closes or stairs with more than twenty flats on each. It had taken him well over an hour but persistent Rory had tracked them down eventually. He had adopted the simple expedient of listening outside each door and, if he heard anything, lifting the letter flap and peering in. As a result, this was the third student party he had been to that night, he said.

Natasha couldn't help laughing at the thought of Rory skulking around, his ears straining for sounds of merriment. It was like a scene from The

Resurrection Men, with Willie Burke waiting in a vennel for anyone who appeared the worse for drink.

They left Leon's after taking a few glasses of wine, and Rory saw Natasha back to her mother's house.

'I'm sorry I can't invite you in, Rory,' she said. 'You understand, it's... well, it's not really my house.'

'Of course, but I'm wanting to see you again tomorrow. Can we meet for lunch?'

'Yes,' she smiled, 'that would be nice.'

For a moment he looked sheepish, then he held her look. Something threatened to overwhelm Natasha as his lips gently brushed hers. She felt his arm around her waist and allowed herself to be held, then gently she pushed him away, smiled, and went into the house.

The next morning Natasha managed to get hold of Kiki on her mobile. She was at Victoria station, just about to board the bus. She would arrive early evening and make her way to the reception.

Natasha took her mother a cup of tea mid-morning, her usual waking time. She seemed more cheerful about the exhibition than Natasha had expected.

'Mum, what exactly is it Semyon does for a living?' Natasha asked.

'He's very influential in cultural circles in the new Russia,' her mother explained. 'He represents a number of artists and performers and makes deals for them in hard currencies. I expect he takes a big cut, but they are grateful to him. Things are terrible over there, you know.'

'So he works for the Russian government?'

'No, he works for an organisation called something like Talent. I'm a bit vague about exactly what it's for. Why don't you ask him? He'll be there tonight.

'Now, darling, I must get up right away.'

'Rory will probably come along tonight, too,' Natasha said. 'Oh, and did I say Kiki's coming up? Is it all right if she stays for a couple of nights?'

'Yes, of course, as long as she can find some space,' her mother said. 'There's a spare room on the top floor, opposite Semyon. I'll leave you to tell her where to find sheets and towels.'

It was a radiant morning with a misty mildness that brought out the best in the city of stone. Natasha made her way past the massive Episcopal cathedral with its three spires, and followed the ornate railings of the Georgian terraces eastwards. Many had private access to lush gardens created out of the hillside, and Natasha heard the tinkle of children's voices and laughter as she walked in their shade.

A bus took her to Princes Street and then up the Mound to cross the Royal Mile. Looking down its colourful length she almost cried out in wonder as her eye caught a haze of blue in the far distance: the Firth of Forth. Why did it all seem so particularly magical to her this morning?

Rory was already at the pub they'd arranged to meet in by the time she arrived. Natasha noticed he was drinking a fruit juice. She ordered the same; there would be plenty to drink later. For now she wanted to have a long and meaningful talk with Rory. Maybe they could walk across the Meadows later; it would be quite perfect.

Unfortunately, it didn't turn out quite so. Since the pub was only around the corner from the college she was continually being recognised by people who would come over and want to know what she had been doing. Then, just as they were becoming a little more intimate, she heard a shout from across the room. It was Kiki, and she struggled out of a rucksack that looked as if it belonged to a commando.

'I'd make a brilliant private dick!' she beamed. 'I just knew this is where I'd find you. Hey, Rory, where did you get that beard?'

Natasha should have guessed that Kiki would know just about everyone in the pub, and soon there was an even greater crowd at their table. By the time they left it was late afternoon, and Natasha remembered she would have to go to the Festival Centre to help with the hanging of her mother's exhibition.

The three of them piled into a taxi and within minutes they were at the top of the Royal Mile. The Hub was a converted gothic church, severe and dark on the outside but a riot of bright colours inside. The exhibition was up an imposing staircase and then into the huge space that was formerly the free Presbyterian church. The carved lectern where the bible readings took place was still in place.

Natasha sensed her mother was relieved to see them. There were still about half the paintings to hang and the reception was at six-thirty. Kiki and Natasha set to work labelling and framing while Rory helped to hang, and in the middle of all this chaos Semyon turned up with a box of wine.

'See, I have managed to find some special vodka,' he announced. 'Compliments of a friend who imports direct. We must drink a toast!'

Eyebrows were raised; would the man not lend a hand? The guests were due in half an hour. And Kiki seemed to be all fingers and thumbs; with a crash she dropped one of the framed watercolours and the glass shattered.

'Oh shit!' she cursed. 'I'm ever so sorry.' And with that she ran, her head buried in her hands, from the hall.

Natasha cleared up the broken shards and then went out in search of her with a worried look at Rory. He smiled encouragingly, indicating that nearly all the pictures were now up.

Kiki was in the ladies putting on some lipstick. She caught sight of Natasha in the mirror and turned to her with the brightest smile. Her eyes shone and she looked vibrant.

'Sorry, Tash,' she apologised. 'I popped my cork out there. I promise to be a good girl for the rest of the evening.'

She arranged her hands in an attitude of prayer and looked heavenwards. Natasha laughed, but it was spooky; only five minutes before she was at breaking point, yet now it was as if she was a different person.

'Tell me more about that scowling Slav who came in,' she went on. 'And then introduce me properly, okay?'

Back out in the main area people were beginning to trickle in. Rory was sweating heavily, standing in one corner, checking that all the pictures were straight. Natasha made straight for him, and could sense he was uneasy.

'Natasha, I think I'll have to go,' he said. 'It looks to be quite a dressy event, and probably not my kind of thing at all.'

She felt it like a punch in the stomach. She had so looked forward to the prospect of being with him. 'But that's not fair, Rory,' she protested. 'I thought you wanted to see the exhibition.'

'I think I've probably looked at it more closely than anyone else in the room, with the exception of your mother,' he pointed out. 'And I explained to her that I would have to leave early, so you don't need to make my excuses for me.'

'I wasn't dreaming of it.' Why was she being so unreasonable, she asked herself?

'Natasha, I'm sorry, but I can't stay for the reception,' he said. 'I just don't feel comfortable dressed like this. Can't you see?'

'Oh, go then,' she sulked.

She watched him leaving and hoped they could maybe make it up again over the next few days before she had to return to London, but she didn't even have his number.

Just then her mobile rang. It was Astrid. A French boutique chain needed a tall dark model for a fashion shoot first thing on Monday, in London. There had been a last minute cancellation. Could Natasha be back by Sunday night? This could be a significant breakthrough for Natasha. The ads would be appearing in a number of high-circulation style and women's magazines.

What was she to do? This might mean she would leave Edinburgh without seeing Rory again, and she'd grown pretty fond of him. But to turn down an opportunity like this was out of the question. Astrid would never forgive her, so with mixed feelings she promised to be back by Sunday.

That night she slept fitfully, dreaming of Rory's strong embrace and then feeling him slip away. She awoke in a sweat, gripping her own arm, then found it difficult to get back to sleep.

Kiki was difficult to rouse from sleep, so it was almost lunchtime before they left the house, after Natasha's mother had promised to pass on her mobile number to anyone who called. Semyon had left earlier, but Kiki had made an arrangement to meet up with him at a gallery near the waterfront in Leith.

Once again she was bright and vivacious after being extremely touchy over breakfast. Natasha was now almost certain that she was on some sort of drugs, but she wondered how Kiki could possibly afford any on a student grant.

They took the bus down Leith Walk and got off near the Scottish Office. There was a thick mist and the view across the Forth was totally obscured. Natasha felt her spirits start to sink.

The gallery was in a converted whisky bond, with low ceilings and rows of cast-iron columns. It reminded Natasha of Jim and the customhouse. He'd never been in touch since that day she had walked out. She had left some clothes behind, but she wasn't going to go back asking for them. And now she seemed to have fallen out with another man, all in the space of a few weeks.

There was Semyon, in a dark suit as usual, talking to a bearded man in jeans. He was introduced to them as the gallery owner. The exhibition was of three Georgian artists, one of them an icon painter. It was brightly coloured, figurative work, highly priced. But even so, few had red stars marking a sale. Saturday morning was always quiet, the bearded man said with a weary smile.

Kiki and Semyon were obviously getting quite a shine off each other. Kiki was once again in the best of spirits, flirting outrageously and expressing an enthusiasm for one of the paintings in particular. She felt Kiki would be happier to have Semyon to herself, so she made an arrangement to meet up with them later, and gratefully left the oppressive atmosphere of the gallery.

Outside it was even more depressing than before, with spits of rain falling on her head. She hadn't come prepared for this, she realised, cursing under her breath. She turned away from the waterfront and almost immediately came across a sign saying, Cleopatra's, over an archway. It led into a tiny courtyard, which gave access to the tall buildings on each side. Cleopatra's was straight ahead, promising a happy hour and snacks. Suddenly she felt in need of a drink and some company to take her out of herself.

The interior was dark, with partitions around the walls and candles on every table. Natasha had ordered a drink before, inspecting her surroundings more closely, she realised that there wasn't a man in the place.

Cleopatra's was girls only!

In a mild panic she gulped at her drink, but there was no way she could just sink it and run; that would be so embarrassing!

So she would just have to try to look inconspicuous.

She noticed that the clientele was divided into those who were wearing fairly conventional summer fashions, and those who were dressed more aggressively in leather and trousers. Feeling extremely uncomfortable, Natasha ordered a bagel and cream cheese, just as a girl approached her who was clearly of the black leather persuasion. A tight-fitting waistcoat with chrome chain attachments at the waist emphasised her petite figure.

'Hi, I've not seen you here before,' the newcomer said brightly. 'Stranger in town?'

'Kind of,' said Natasha. 'I was brought up here, but I left a year ago to live in London.'

Immediately the other girl was all ears, wanting to

hear about the lesbian scene in Soho. Natasha could either make it all up or admit ignorance, so she decided, partly out of devilment, to do the former. After all, her time at the Academy had opened her eyes.

The girl introduced herself as Phoebe, and offered to buy the drinks. She seemed friendly enough, so where could the harm be in Natasha chatting for a while? She was a little strange looking, her dark hair cut in a suede effect crop, and a silver stud glittered in her nose.

In fact, the chat turned out to be nearer two hours. Natasha had to be very careful how she made up the story of her lesbian experiences, so she used the incidents from the Academy and saw with satisfaction how Phoebe's eyes widened. Gaining confidence, she embellished on her experiences with Fiona at the photo shoot, but this time making it sound as if it were all her idea.

They were sitting close and soon Phoebe's heavily ringed fingers settled on Natasha's thigh. Natasha was becoming confused as the drink began to take effect. More women came to join them, and she found herself part of a small crowd gathered in the courtyard. Looking up, she could see a patch of blue sky framed by the buildings.

Four or five women were all talking and laughing at once, most of them well on in the drinks department. What else could they all do except continue where they had left off? It felt like the easiest thing in the world to go with them to someone's flat, so Natasha staggered along slightly on the cobbles. Phoebe took her arm and they leaned against each other as they went.

The next instant they were on a common staircase lit all the way up by glass bricks. It was like climbing through the air, spiralling upwards. Then they all piled through a door and into a big living room with two sofas. Almost immediately music was blasting out and dancing started.

The heavy beat and throbbing sensuality of the songs made Natasha extra sensitive to the bodies of the women around her. Three of them were dancing, another two were petting on one of the sofas. One had already unzipped her jeans and was pulling them down as the other held her face between her hands in a long kiss. Natasha tried not to stare.

A tall blonde with a sensational figure, wearing a tight black dress with a plunging top, joined the two in their passionate embrace. Giggling, they both reached down to the hem of her dress and suddenly peeled it up. With the advantage of surprise it was quickly high enough to expose her breasts. Underneath she was wearing nothing. Her breasts were full and proud, and her stomach toned.

One of them whispered something in her ear, inaudible against the plaintive wail of the music. Then, as Natasha and Phoebe looked on, the blonde raised her arms and the dress was slipped over her head and thrown to one side, and she made no attempt to conceal her lovely nakedness.

She looked Natasha straight in the eye as her friends fondled her breasts, one of them gently flicking the coral tip with her tongue. Still she held Natasha's gaze, her eyes shining, her shoulders swaying alluringly to the music. Then the controlling hands began to explore her more audaciously, circling her hips and gently probing between her thighs. She would soon be totally in their control, she must have known, but she seemed determined to postpone that delicious moment for as long as she could. Natasha watched her eyes begin to mist over. Then, with a final look that seemed to bid Natasha farewell, the blonde threw her head back and her mouth formed a soundless scream of pleasure. She ineffectually tried to push the hands away, as if the pleasure was too intense, but it was too late to free herself from the snare of her own desire. One girl knelt before her, while the other adopted a neck-lock from behind, gently forcing her head down and pinning her forearms. The blonde tensed as the girl kneeling in front went down on her with a probing tongue.

Phoebe pulled at Natasha's arm. 'Come on, let's split and leave them to it,' she whispered.

They left, Natasha's head in a whirl, and not just from the drink. She felt strongly drawn to little Phoebe, with her forthright yet chirpy attitude. She could see the way things were heading, and her inner desire was asserting itself. But was she really going to do something like she'd just witnessed with another woman, and a virtual stranger?

Natasha had expected Phoebe's flat to be some distance away, but when they reached the ground floor she produced a key and opened the door on the right, motioning Natasha inside. As soon as the door was closed behind them, Phoebe reached up and took Natasha's face gently in both hands. The warmth on her cheeks and the girl's pleading look combined to overwhelm Natasha's reason, and they joined in a passionate, lingering kiss.

Then Phoebe stepped back and her hands went up to the top of her studded leather waistcoat. She unzipped it to the waist and, taking Natasha's hand, pulled it in and held it against the faint swell of one of her breasts. Under her touch Natasha felt its tip begin to harden. She also felt the increasing of her own arousal and a familiar melting between her thighs. She sighed as Phoebe's hands began to probe under her T-shirt.

Feverishly, before she thought better of it, she pulled the garment over her head and then undid her bra. Phoebe, smiling with pleasure, immediately reached out and lightly pinched one nipple between thumb and forefinger. Then she held out a hand and drew Natasha through into the bedroom.

During the next few hours Phoebe inhabited Natasha's world both physically and imaginatively, giving her the most extreme pleasure Natasha imagined it was possible for anyone to receive. Initially she felt shame, but soon it evaporated. At one point she heard the muffled ring of her mobile, stuffed into her bag in the hallway. Was it Rory? She should have jumped up to answer, but little Phoebe's hot breath at her ear warned her not to think of it.

They both fell asleep and it was dark when Natasha awoke to the smell of cooking. Phoebe was making an omelette. It seemed only good manners to accept the thoughtful offer, and besides, she was ravenous. Wrapped in Phoebe's dressing gown, she balanced the plate on her thighs whilst sitting cross-legged on the floor. They began to talk again over coffee, and they got on so well together it seemed a pity that she had to return to London. Natasha felt torn – rootless even. Looking at her watch, she realised it was already Sunday, early morning. It was too late to find a bus, and she didn't have a very clear idea of exactly where she was anyway.

Even as she was turning this over in her mind, Phoebe moved towards her. She was wearing only a singlet, her tiny breasts just visible beneath the white cotton. She gently parted Natasha's knees and squatted between them, then without taking her eyes off Natasha's, produced from behind her back a hank of cord and a black leather collar. She let them swing together from her raised hand, and Natasha held her gaze without flinching, knowing immediately what was to come. She couldn't resist, so she nodded slowly and, leaning back, let the gown slip from her shoulders.

Phoebe buckled the collar around Natasha's throat. It was soft, with a small ring at the front. She was otherwise naked. Skilfully, Phoebe bound together one wrist and ankle, and then the other as Natasha knelt with her back to the sofa. She was made helpless, but Phoebe's touch was quite unlike Jim's during the only bondage sessions she had previously experienced. The girl showed a tenderness in her mastery, whilst leaving Natasha in no doubt who was the dominant party.

She stroked the insides of Natasha's thighs, running her fingers closer and closer to the seat of her pleasure, making her desperate with anticipation. If only she was free she would grasp Phoebe's hands and guide them to where she so desperately needed them to be.

But her lover was stoking her fires slowly, making her wait for the flames to catch and spread. She grinned mischievously as she saw the effect she was having. Natasha's head lolled back and she closed her eyes, savouring the expert touch between her legs, preparing for ecstasy.

It was ordained.

Then she felt herself being pushed back and down firmly until her spine would bend no more and her shoulders were pinned to the sofa, her silky hair spread out on the cushions. With one hand moulding Natasha's firm breasts, Phoebe began to fondle her pussy with the other, easing a finger between her moistening lips, slippery with the intensity of her arousal. Cooing encouragement, Phoebe began to grope Natasha with more emphasis, still holding her down, bound and spread before her like a helpless sacrifice.

Phoebe leaned closer and whispered obscenities into Natasha's ear. She thought she would scream with pent-up passion if Phoebe did not release her, and the crude intentions whispered in hushed tones only fuelled the breathless intensity of her arousal. She could neither stretch her legs nor reciprocate with her hands. Phoebe's pleasure was to have total control over the intensity of hers.

The awareness of Natasha's precarious situation seemed to heighten her appetite for more and more. Brushing the hair from Natasha's perspiring brow, Phoebe brought her pale lips into predatory contact with Natasha's. Her tongue probed deep, making their kiss into a wildly sensual echo of the manipulation being undertaken between her thighs.

By now Phoebe had inserted four fingers into her, stretching her vagina walls. The punk girl would not, could not, be denied. Natasha felt herself go completely limp, almost into a faint, as the waves of delight engulfed her. Again and again they came, but each time Phoebe was there with her, forcing their lips together and kissing her deeply. Why, Natasha wondered through a haze of sheer bliss, was it so much more intense when she felt so helpless?

When she awoke the languorous aftermath of their lovemaking still remained. Her wrists bore the faintly blue marks of the cord. She looked at her watch, and realised with a sickening start that the London coach would be leaving in just over an hour!

There was no sign of Phoebe, so she guessed she

must have gone out for the Sunday papers.

On the mobile she talked to her mother and to Kiki as she took a taxi. She explained she had to be back at the Academy in order to make the modelling assignment.

'I don't think I can, Tash,' said Kiki, in response to Natasha's question as to whether she'd be travelling back south with her. 'I've made an arrangement with Semyon that we'd go to the surrealist exhibition after lunch. I'm really sorry, Tash. I can't call it off, but I will see you later in the week.'

'So are you staying up here tomorrow as well?' Natasha asked.

'Yeah, probably. Semyon's got plans. Anyway, where were you last night?' she added, changing the subject.

Why didn't she tell Kiki the truth? If she couldn't tell her best friend, who could she tell? But no, she said she'd been with Rory. And she felt that Kiki was hiding something about her relationship with Semyon.

Thoughts such as these occupied her mind during the return journey. And then she relived the wonderful night with Phoebe, feeling guilty that she had to run off without saying goodbye.

And still there was no call from Rory.

It was around nine o'clock when the taxi pulled up in the driveway of the Academy. She pushed open the large front door and heaved her case in behind her. It was strangely quiet. Usually there were girls around the place, some of them just back from a weekend at home.

Just then Jean came down the stairs, took one look of horror at Natasha, and then turned tail and bounded back up the way she'd come. Leaving her case, Natasha went in pursuit, her curiosity aroused.

For some reason she had a feeling deep inside that she knew her destination as she pursued the fleeing figure along the landing. And sure enough, she caught up with Jean just outside her own bedroom door. Simpering pathetically the girl tried to twist from her grasp, but Natasha had no reason to waste time on her, so she pushed her aside, gripped the handle, took a deep breath, and thrust the door open.

Her jaw dropped in surprise. Whatever she had imagined, it had been nothing like this.

Evelyn Marnie was sitting straight-backed on the edge of her bed. Over her lap sprawled a figure, a mass of blonde hair covering her face and almost reaching down to the carpet. Evelyn, recovering herself quickly after the abrupt disturbance, smiled slyly, still holding the struggling figure firmly across her lap.

The sobbing figure's buttocks were bared and flaming red, clearly visible even as she tried to reach back and place her hands protectively over them. She whimpered, clearly anticipating further punishment. In Evelyn's hand was the black leather tawse Natasha had once before seen through the keyhole. The poor blonde slowly lifted her head to look at Natasha, her eyes tearful, a picture of misery and humiliation.

'Saffron!' Natasha exclaimed. 'What...? I don't understand.'

Evelyn cut in sharply. 'No, Natasha, my dear, you don't understand... yet. But you will.'

With that Evelyn stood up, dismissively rolling Saffron to the floor, where she lay in a heap. Natasha moved to comfort her as Evelyn Marnie straightened her skirt and briskly left the room, slamming the door behind her.

Chapter 8

Natasha just couldn't go on like this. Coming to the Academy had looked just the right move when she first met Astrid. Now it just seemed to have added to the uncertainties she felt about her life.

She slept badly and woke late. It turned out Saffron was more affronted than upset. She didn't seem to be concerned so much about the punishment, after a run-in over something to do with smoking in her room, more that Natasha had burst in and caught her in such an embarrassing situation.

And today was a big day. This was Natasha's first real modelling assignment. She had arranged to meet up with Astrid after lunch and she would go with her to the run through in the ballroom of a Mayfair hotel. A French fashion house called Risqué was launching a younger version of its couture range. This was to be an evening for trade buyers from some of the more upmarket dress shops and boutiques. Gloss, the agency, had lost one of their girls to a rival at the last moment, and one of their bookers had contacted Astrid in desperation. They needed a more exotic look, and she had seen what they were looking for in Natasha's portfolio.

The ballroom of the venue was exceptionally grand, with three huge ornate chandelier overhead and pier-glass mirrors around the walls reflecting a kaleidoscope of shifting colours. There was a buzz about the place as the final touches were being put to the long raised catwalk. Tables were also being laid with red check tablecloths. The show was to take place after the guests had enjoyed some typical French cuisine.

'Astrid, there you are!' A small effervescent

middle-aged woman with a round face and bright red hair approached and air-kissed. To her surprise, Natasha received the same welcome after being introduced by Astrid. The woman was Zoë, the top talent scout at Gloss. She stood back and nodded approvingly at Natasha.

'Oh yes, you're just what we're looking for,' she decided enthusiastically. 'Are you feeling nervous, Natasha? Don't be overawed by this place. Risqué said they wanted somewhere that had a touch of Versailles to it, and this was the nearest thing I could find after the French embassy. They weren't too keen on the idea, as you might imagine. This is costing a packet, so let's hope we get the turnout.'

Natasha felt the woman would have talked away quite happily for a long time, even though there must have been hundreds of things still to be done before the show opened.

At last Zoë took her away to see behind the scenes. It was reminiscent of her first time at the charity catwalk show, but this time there was far more people and even greater mayhem. She was introduced to a string of people from make-up and hair to seamstresses and stage technicians. It was very bewildering, but also tremendously exciting. She tried to take an interest in everything that was going on.

Zoë left her to go and find the other girls. Natasha was sitting on the end of the catwalk in some apprehension. She had seen her outfits and was thrilled. Many of them were dresses and playsuits in cashmere mixes, as well as some leather skirts and coats, plus some beautiful satin blouses with hipsters. She couldn't wait to try them all on.

A chorus of shouts and laughter came from behind the curtain, then red-haired Zoë emerged with a broad smile on her round face and five or six girls in tow. Most were probably a year or so younger than Natasha, but one she guessed to be around her own age. They all trooped down the catwalk in high spirits, one or two sashaying out of habit.

Zoë introduced them and they all gave Natasha a hug. Then it was time to do the run through with lights and music, and Natasha watched the other girls with a keen interest. Although younger than her, they of course had more catwalk experience, but her advantages included a greater maturity and a better self-awareness. She noticed, for example, that when they stepped out on the catwalk some had blank expressions, whilst others had the fixed smile of a prima ballerina. She would try for something more natural, communicating a feeling that would in some way complement the garment she was wearing.

The run through went off well. Thierry Murger, the designer dressed in matched blues from his tinted shades to his loafers, seemed happy. Anyway, he was chatting animatedly to Zoë and she was smiling broadly. Seeing Natasha sitting on her own, she gave her a wink.

Natasha was approached by Mila, a stunning ash-blonde with perfectly oval eyes and face, the older girl of the group. The models were taking a snack break before hair and make-up got started at seven. Mila asked Natasha to wait while she went to freshen up, but after ten minutes or so Natasha was getting impatient with waiting.

Entering the ladies she realised something was happening. Mila and two others were grouped around the marble top to the basins. One of them was standing facing the mirror with a knuckle pressed below her nose, as if to stop herself from sneezing. The others were smiling broadly at her, and they all turned as one as Natasha entered.

'Oh, Natasha, sorry to keep you!' gushed Mila. 'We were just completing our... um... preparations for tonight. We're all going to take a look at the salad bar up on the first floor. Okay by you?' With that, she deftly squashed a few remaining grains of white on the black surface and rubbed her forefinger against her upper teeth. She grimaced.

'Waste not, want not,' a black girl said sarcastically, and they picked up their bags and trooped out, Natasha in their wake. She'd heard that drugs were endemic in the fashion world, and she was learning fast.

But she had little time to think more about it, as events conspired to rush her off her feet. As they returned to the ballroom Risqué's guests were beginning to arrive. Natasha felt her pulse quicken in anticipation.

For the next hour or so Natasha and the others would be in the hands of the make-up girls, and must be prepared to have one side of their faces transformed into a playing card. When she first heard of Thierry's notion of a pack of cards she thought it crazy, but now she could see it would introduce the right note of humour and irreverence.

Thank goodness she wasn't the joker. That was Mila, but she didn't seem to mind, her right cheek adorned with a brightly coloured cap and bells. She was alert and bright-eyed as they waited behind the curtain for Zoë to open the show, as soon as coffee was served. Natasha felt the anticipation of the girls around her. It was not that different, come to think of it, from the atmosphere at the opening night of The Resurrection Men. She already felt part of the team.

And it all went like a dream. The first sight of the

catwalk stretching out in front of her, traversed by racing spots of intensely coloured light, was hugely disconcerting. But Natasha gathered her resolve, relaxed her body and absorbed the beat of the amplified track. Then she stepped out, swaying slightly to the rhythm, and smiled with sheer pleasure at the sensation of being the focus of so much attention.

Natasha was in a world of her own. Out there were others, possibly hostile, with their own opinions of her. But in her mind she was safe, as if she were walking on a pier of solid masonry stretching further and further into a stormy sea.

At the end of the evening Thierry Murger approached her. He complimented her performance and told her to take away with her any garment she liked. Natasha's head spun; it was like living a dream. She had a hard choice to make, but eventually opted for the salmon-coloured playsuit.

'That will suit you well, Natasha,' he said. 'I'm sorry you did not have the chance to wear it during the show. Still, there will be other shows in the future, let us hope.'

Natasha could only smile and blush like a schoolgirl.

She returned with Astrid in her car, and still hadn't woken from the dream. Saying goodnight, she jumped from the car at the front gate. It was very late, and she didn't expect anyone to be up.

But as she approached the front door she saw a faint glow from the library window, as if a light were on in the hall and the door was left partly open. She was sure she could see the outline of a tall figure in the window. Looking out for her? Then she saw Evelyn's car parked in the dark under a tree, and felt a shiver of apprehension dampen her elation.

When she let herself in Natasha was immediately aware of a presence. And sure enough, the light clicked on and there was Evelyn framed in the door to the library. Her raven hair was loose, down to her shoulders, and she sported a brittle smile.

'Natasha, you look quite radiant,' she said. 'I don't need to ask if tonight was a success; it's written all over your face. I'm only sorry I couldn't be there to see it for myself.'

'I'm sorry too, Evelyn,' Natasha said diplomatically. She had no idea of the reason for Evelyn not being at the show, but playing the Cinderella card was not going to win her any sympathy. She knew only too well the scheming and domineering streak Evelyn possessed, and was determined not to fall victim to it again.

'Why don't you come up to my room, and you can tell me all about it over a nice cup of coffee?' Evelyn suggested tightly. 'I've been waiting here for your return, so how about it?'

Already she was sidling closer. True, Natasha had recently savoured her time with Phoebe, but the thought of Evelyn's touch was enough to make her flesh crawl, so she turned her down with the minimum of politeness.

Evelyn lowered her eyes, but when she looked up again they were blazing. 'Don't try and cross me, Natasha,' she hissed. 'Just remember what I said to you before. You are within my total control while you are under this roof. I am genuinely glad your career is taking off, but don't think because of that you will ever get the better of me!'

Natasha tried to hold her ground as the woman stormed past her, the mere ferocity of the outburst making her knees weaken.

The Risqué event had been a stroke of luck for Natasha, and very soon she heard from Astrid that she was required again. Thierry had asked especially for her to model the same range, but this time to French buyers. She would need to go to Paris for three wonderful days!

Unfortunately, once the word got around a number of the girls became very hostile, out of envy. Even Saffron seemed far less friendly than before. Natasha began to feel quite depressed, even though the visit to Paris was only weeks away. She spent more time away from the Academy than before, usually over at Kiki's flat. There she soon became aware that Kiki was seeing Semyon since returning from Edinburgh. She also found out that he was supplying her with considerably more than just romance. Kiki bridled when Natasha tried to find out more.

'Oh, stop sounding like my mother, Tash!' she exploded. 'I'm not hooked on crack, it's just my way of loosening up and getting into my art. Semyon has a good source of supply and he lets me have some once in a while, that's all.'

'My God, Kiki, do you know where he gets it from? Have you no idea the danger you could be in if he used it as a lever to persuade you to... well, to do things.'

'What kind of things exactly were you thinking of?' Kiki snapped. 'I'm not just off the banana boat, you know. If I smell a rat, I'll bid Semyon a fond farewell. Okay, momma dearest? Anyway, how are you making out with Rory?'

'He's still not contacted me,' Natasha admitted. 'I think I just pissed him off by sulking at the art exhibition. It's my own stupid fault, I realise that now.'

'Oh come on, he's not worth ruining your eyeliner for,' Kiki said, her temper ebbing quickly. 'I'll tell you what, I think I've got a mutual acquaintance in Edinburgh. I'll try and find out from him what Rory's up to. Think of me as your private dick, Tash, okay? I'll have a report for you when you get back from Paris. By then you'll probably have loads of other men on your mind, you lucky monkey!'

Paris was just as wonderful as Kiki told her it would be. The evening Natasha arrived there was a bus tour that took her past the Louvre and the Invalides, all lit up spectacularly, and then over the Seine to see the Eiffel Tower, its iron tracery launching itself into the night sky like a rocket. Then there was the stately drive up the Champs Elysées to the Arc de Triomphe. It was like being part of a fairytale.

Natasha was seated next to Mila. She was trying hard to show that she was not overwhelmed at what Paris had to offer; too hard, thought Natasha. Then, after a longish absence in the coach toilet, she seemed distinctly brighter. Natasha remembered the gathering in the ladies toilet at the fashion show and put two and two together.

Behind them was Luc, who was supposed to be their guide. He was known as a PR, standing for personal relations, Natasha was told. There were other less polite abbreviations she was told about too. Up to now Luc had been preoccupied with the two young French models, sitting across the aisle. Now, his dark hair shaved close to the skull and with a brass ring in one ear, he came and sat in front of Mila and Natasha and turned to face them. He paused and then smiled shyly.

'Hello, I am Luc,' he said. 'This is your first time here in Paris, I believe? You must permit me to show you the sights during the daytime as well.'

'I don't know if we're going to have any spare time while we're here.' Mila responded with a dismissive look, but Natasha knew it was just a ploy. Luc was nothing special to look at, but he had persistence. He wasn't going to be put off by a sulky show, and knew how to use his boyish charm.

Natasha knew the reputation of the PR's who chaperoned the younger models. They were supposed to make sure they didn't get lost or fall into the clutches of any unsuitable men. All the agencies used them, but in some cases the PR's turned out to be little more than pimps. Anyway, by the time the coach had put them down at their hotel on the left bank opposite Nôtre Dame, Mila was looking vivacious and her body language was unmistakable.

It was no surprise that she didn't come up to their twin room immediately. Natasha was exhausted and getting a little tired of Mila's mood swings, and so she gave the two of them a grateful wave as they headed for a bistro that Luc had recommended highly for a night-cap, leaving her alone to relax.

The following morning she could hardly rouse Mila, but fortunately they weren't needed for rehearsals until the afternoon. So, after a quick breakfast of crumbly brioche and aromatic coffee Natasha made a decision; she would take off to see a little of Paris on her own. She was told that a bus was the best way to see the streets and she received help from the concierge who recommended a visit to Montmartre – the quartier de bohème, as he put it.

She was deeply entranced by what she saw that morning. From the steep cobbled streets with their overhanging balconies and window boxes to the wonderful range of food shops offering delicacies that she did not recognise and hesitated to guess what they might be made of. Everything seemed designed to enchant.

It felt so strange and exciting, maybe even slightly frightening since her French was still limited, and she often had difficulty remembering which way to look when she stepped off the pavement. Yes, this was the bohemian quarter all right. Wherever she looked, pasted onto walls or displayed on glass-covered notice boards were posters and leaflets offering courses in painting, design and drawing. She knew they would be the same kind of courses Kiki was doing in London, but sights and sounds seemed so much more exotic in Paris.

Extraordinary words turned out, with the help of her pocket dictionary, to have quite mundane meanings. Here was one right in front of her, Metropolitain, spelt out in elongated lettering on the most extraordinary canopy of glass and green-painted ironwork she had ever seen. The front stuck out at roof level like the peak of a baseball cap, and the uprights supporting it looked like slender trees.

Indeed, this particular one was surrounded by trees, and there was a group of stalls selling the kind of things she would buy in Camden Market. Natasha tried to ask the girl selling candles what it was, but all she could do was indicate that Natasha should go down the steps. She descended, and realised immediately that this was the underground system. Luc had told them it was very efficient, so she tried to work out how best to get back to her hotel. But since she had forgotten the name of the nearest metro station it was a hopeless task.

It was almost lunchtime and time to find the return bus and make her way back. But this was easier said than done. She got on the bus going in quite the wrong direction to start with, and when she had boarded the right bus it seemed to travel desperately slowly, in traffic that was getting heavier as they moved nearer the city centre.

She called the hotel number on her mobile and got through to Mila, who cheerfully informed her that the minibus was about to leave for the rehearsal. She said she would pass on a message about her to one of the PR's, but Natasha wasn't sure whether she would or not.

So when, half an hour later, she jumped off the bus and ran the few metres to the hotel it was with relief that she saw Luc waiting in the foyer. He gave his shy smile and took her hand.

'Natasha, you are here at last,' he said.

'I got lost and took the wrong bus,' she explained. 'I'm so sorry.'

'Do not worry so much,' he soothed calmly. 'I will get you to the theatre very soon, but have you had anything to eat?'

They went around the corner to a pâtisserie and he bought her a baguette filled with slices of delicious cheese and red lettuce.

He then took her arm and, whirling her around, walked over to an impressive white car parked at the kerb. Removing the parking ticket dismissively, he motioned for her to get in.

Luc drove fast, but sensing that he was a capable driver, Natasha relaxed and enjoyed the baguette.

'Where are we going, Luc?' she asked between mouthfuls.

'To the Musée des Papillons,' he told her. 'You understand? It is an exposition of papillons.'

She was about to dive for her pocket dictionary, when Luc took both hands off the wheel to make swooping motions with thumbs crossed. She had to work it out fast or they would surely crash.

'Butterflies?' she said. 'Yes, I understand, Luc. It's a place that specialises in butterfly collections. Yes?'

They swung off the road and through a pair of tall gates with a stone lion set on a plinth to one side. It was a kind of park. Luc swung the car along a winding driveway and they were suddenly in front of an imposing looking mansion with a number of vehicles parked outside, including a minibus that Natasha recognised.

'Nous voici,' she said under her breath.

'Très bien parlé, ma jolie!' he turned and smiled at her, and she coloured with pride at his compliment.

The show went well. The French audience was more enthusiastic than the London audience. Thierry was mobbed by a group of adoring women buyers, and several approached Natasha and said things she took to be complimentary. She just said, 'Anglaise,' and then only one stayed to try out her halting English.

Then there was the mandatory outing to a nightclub, where they stayed until well into the morning, listening to a female chanteuse with a smoker's growl crooning songs of the lovelorn. Natasha felt herself drifting back into a dreamworld. This was it! She was really part of this charmed circle!

On one occasion, when she visited the toilets, she came out of the stall to find Mila bent with her head over a basin. For a minute Natasha thought she was retching, but then she saw the traces of white powder.

Mila rubbed her nose with the back of a finger. 'Just what the doctor ordered,' she gasped.

'I really doubt it, Mila,' said Natasha. 'How long have you had the habit?'

'You mean, when did I start?' she scoffed. 'No idea, darling. It's just one of the qualifications for this job.' She laughed harshly, but her face was sad. 'Believe me, the money isn't everything. It's stressful, you know, always having to look perfection, and at my age I'm beginning to feel like I'm on the way out.'

Natasha nodded sympathetically. 'I can imagine how it could be,' she said. 'But you're only a little older than I am, Mila. Now you're established and you've still got years. I'd really love to be getting to see the world and earning fabulous money. I'm just not sure I've got what it takes.'

'Don't worry, darling,' Mila said. 'You've got it in spades. With those Slavic looks you're a natural. Thierry more or less told you that at the London show, didn't he?'

'I suppose so,' Natasha conceded. 'Well, he said he hoped to see me again, and then out of the blue Zoë booked me for this.'

'Well then, you're on the high road, girl. My advice is to make the most of it. Gloss is one of the best in the business. If you really want to work for them you can do it. If you do well here the word will get straight back to Zoë. They'll book you in for the spring shows early next year, and the rumour is they're going to open a Paris bureau.'

'But I'm not on their books yet,' Natasha pointed out. 'I'm still at the Academy.'

'I should pack that in pronto, Natasha. There's nothing more they can teach you. Get real, it's for kids straight out of nursery school.'

Just as Mila predicted, within a few days of returning to London Natasha received a call from Zoë's secretary.

Over a light salad lunch in a hotel in Belgravia Zoë made it clear that Gloss would like to represent Natasha, but she would have to be available in time for the main European catwalk shows.

'Natasha, I'd heard your agreement with the Academy expires soon,' Zoë said. 'That means that in a few weeks you're free of any obligations to Astrid. This is a great opportunity, believe me. We would send you over to Paris for a month initially, to see how you coped.'

'I'd feel I'm letting Astrid down,' Natasha protested. 'I'll need some time to think about it. But please don't imagine for a moment I'm not grateful for your interest in me.'

'Of course, darling, you need to be quite confident you're making the right decision,' Zoë sympathised. 'But you can't stay with Astrid forever if you want to make your way in fashion. And from what I hear, you're starting to be bankable. Believe me, Astrid's already recouped her investment in you. Anything else would be super profits. Believe me, Natasha, I know this business, and we all need to move fast.'

Later that week Natasha went round to Kiki's for a chat.

'Hiya stranger, and before I forget,' Kiki gabbled, 'I've got some news that should make you pee your pants.'

'Oh?'

'Tash, you really look as if butter wouldn't melt in your pussy,' Kiki giggled. 'I know you're simply gagging to know.'

For a moment Natasha couldn't make out just what Kiki was on about. She seemed highly excited. Natasha tried to look eager as a leaf of sketchpad was dangled in front of her nose. On it there was a crude portrait in charcoal which, thanks to the evidence of beard on his chin, she just about recognised as Rory. Underneath was a phone number, and she embraced her friend with genuine gratitude.

'I'm going back to Edinburgh for the Christmas period, and maybe New Year,' she told her friend. 'I hope he'll be around. Do you want to come?'

'Something tells me I'm going to be in the way if you do make contact with Rory,' Kiki said. 'By the way, that's his flat phone number. My contact didn't have his mobile. Anyway, Semyon is being very mysterious about something he has planned for us over the holiday period.'

'Oh Kiki, do you think he's taking you to Russia?' Natasha squealed excitedly. 'Are you getting on okay, then?'

'What do you think?' Kiki looked very pleased with herself. She twirled, making the tunic ripple sensuously, but then she staggered slightly and for a second her eyes seemed a little unfocussed.

'Semyon bought it for you?' Natasha asked, dismissing the lapse. 'You are a lucky girl!'

She settled down with a vodka blush that Kiki prepared in an instant. She needed to get on to her problems.

'Kiki,' she went on, 'I've been offered a contract by a modelling agency that will take me to Paris. What do you think? It will mean leaving the Academy before Christmas, and I think Astrid will be upset. Oh, and where am I going to put my stuff? I can't take it all to Paris with me.'

'You're being such a goose, Natasha!' Kiki snorted. 'This must be the opportunity of a lifetime, and you're considering turning down the chance to go and live in Paris and tread the catwalks of

Europe. Your head must be turning to mince if you swither over this one.'

By the time Natasha had dragged herself back to the Academy, Kiki had persuaded her to go with Gloss. But she couldn't face having to tell Astrid that she was leaving. Zoë congratulated her on making the right decision, and said a six-month contract would soon be in the post. She reassured Natasha about telling Astrid, and even offered to do it for her.

Sure enough, the agreement arrived, committing Natasha to starting with the agency the second week in January. She would get a fixed salary plus a performance-related top-up. She would move immediately to the Paris bureau and Gloss would provide accommodation and PR escorts if required. She signed without any further hesitation.

The remaining time until the end of the Academy session dragged on. Natasha was worried that Astrid hadn't asked her in for a chat about her future, but on the other hand, she was abroad for a while. And Natasha was out almost every day doing product promotions in the big stores, work that rapidly became tedious.

In the evenings she had Evelyn to contend with, always suggesting little get-togethers in her room. All in all Natasha decided not to tell anyone about Gloss. After all, once the six months was up she didn't need to give notice. Her farewell was to be a surprise.

The final evening was to be the Academy's farewell soirée. Everyone knew Saffron was leaving to work for an agency that specialised in catalogue photo shoots. The usual thing was for leavers to give short farewell performances. Saffron was doing a short dance number and Natasha had decided to recite something in French. She had settled on a poem by Mallarmé.

Zoë was one of the guests at the soirée, and she immediately embraced Natasha upon her arrival.

'Hiya, honey!' she gushed. 'How's it going? Are you all ready for Paris?'

'Zoë, I'm worried that Astrid hasn't said anything to me about terminating my stay,' Natasha admitted, her brow furrowed. 'Not a word. You did tell her, didn't you?'

'Don't worry, honey. She knows. I sent her a letter two weeks ago. She's probably just had her nose put out a tad.'

'But that's the week she was abroad. I really don't think she got it, Zoë.'

'Surely her assistant would have dealt with her correspondence, and put it on one side for her to read when she came back?'

Natasha suddenly had a sick feeling in the pit of her stomach. She watched Zoë go over to talk with Astrid, and then she sensed Astrid's piercing blue eyes single her out from the crowd. Then she stormed straight through a group of girls in party hats to where Natasha stood, her face pale with fury.

'So, this is how you treat my generosity?' she spat viciously. 'What do you mean by going behind my back, young lady?'

Natasha was aware that the hubbub of voices had died down. 'Astrid, this isn't at all how it looks. Phoebe said she'd told you, so I didn't think I needed to say anything. I was expecting you to approach me—'

'I was planning to do exactly that after the Christmas break,' Astrid interrupted. 'It shouldn't have escaped your notice that I've been in Italy and France. As it happens, I was looking out for catwalk opportunities for you and the other girls, but it would seem I busted a gut for nothing!'

'I... I'm really sorry, Astrid,' Natasha blurted guiltily. 'I just thought you knew.'

'And I thought you realised that I was counting on you for the spring fashion shows. Well, if that's how you feel, there are plenty of girls here who I'm sure will jump at the chance.'

Astrid turned on her heel and left Natasha open-mouthed, clutching the paperback Mallarmé edition in both hands for comfort.

Saffron came over to give her some support. 'Natasha, jolly well done,' she enthused. 'I had a feeling you were heading off somewhere after that trip to Paris. But why did you keep it such a secret?'

'I wanted it to be a surprise. Honestly, Saffron, there was nothing more to it. I just thought...'

'You just thought you would have your own little secret that you could keep from the rest of us?' Evelyn cut in, appearing from nowhere. She made the observation with her grimmest smile. She was dressed in a daringly short black leather skirt and a lavender top with lacy cuffs. Noticing the book of poetry, she changed the subject and asked to see it.

'I didn't realise that you were an admirer of decadent fin de siècle poetry, Natasha.'

'I didn't realise they were decadent,' Natasha retorted. 'I was going to recite one of them at the soirée. I thought it would be... appropriate.' She realised how stupid that sounded, and wished she had kept quiet about the whole idea.

Evelyn's eyebrows were arched in amusement. 'Why, my dear girl, what a splendid idea! Do you want to go before or after Saffron?'

'Um, well, after would be fine, I suppose,' she said. 'So could I have the book back please?'

'But I thought you said you were going to recite to us?'

'Yes, but I thought with the book, in case... well, in case I have a lapse of memory.'

'Oh, but I am sure you won't,' the woman said effusively. 'And anyway, my dear, I can act as prompter. Just tell me the title of the poem you've chosen and we'll make a fine partnership, I'm sure.'

Evelyn went off to make the final preparations for the soirée, and Natasha was left to wait in nervous anticipation as chairs were arranged in rows. She noticed Astrid having a word with Evelyn before leaving with Zoë. Soon there was a hush as Evelyn stood by the piano to address the guests.

Saffron danced beautifully with a piano accompaniment from Jean, but Natasha couldn't concentrate as she ran through the words of the poem in her head. Messangère, or was it Messagerie?

'Next we have our other leaver, Natasha, a surprise to most of us but nonetheless we shall be sorry to see her go,' Evelyn announced. 'Natasha has landed a contract with Gloss, and will be working in Paris for the spring shows.'

Natasha heard whispered taunts from Chloe and her·cronies as she stepped forward in front of the grand piano. Clasping her hands together in front of her to try and hide her nervousness, she started off as best she could.

Soon she realised with increasing panic that she was not going to get past the third verse. It was as if she was surrounded by darkness and the battery in her torch was failing.

'No, Natasha, that's not right. You should have said mésangette, it means a birdcage. Go back to the first line of the verse and try again.' Evelyn's crisp pronunciation made her realise how miserable her rendition must have sounded. Once again she stumbled on the words and Evelyn had to come to her rescue. This time, however, there was more menace in her tone.

'Come on, Natasha, you can surely do better than this.' She read the verse through with faultless intonation, the book half closed, showing that she had memorised it in minutes.

'I'm sorry Evelyn, and everybody in the audience, but I'm afraid I just can't remember the rest,' Natasha apologised meekly. 'Maybe if you could let me have the book back, Evelyn?'

There were sniggers from some of the girls.

'Not just yet, Natasha,' the woman denied her. 'I'm confident of your powers of recall, but maybe you need an aide-memoire?'

Natasha relaxed slightly with relief. 'Oh, yes please,' she said.

More sniggers.

'Good, and I am more than ready to supply it,' Evelyn stated.

With a flourish she produced the black leather riding crop with the scarlet tab, the very same which Natasha had previously spied her using on Chloe. A concerted gasp went through the watching girls and guests as Evelyn strode to the front, slapping it against her leather covered thigh.

'Now, Natasha, you have one last chance to redeem yourself,' she announced. 'Give me the third stanza of Sagesse word perfect please.'

She laid the crop emphatically on the lustrously polished piano top, within easy reach, and consulted the book. Natasha's mind raced, individual French phrases and lines lying tantalisingly just beyond her powers of recall. She closed her eyes and prayed this would all prove to be nothing more than a nightmare when she opened them.

But the next thing she saw when she opened them was Evelyn with the crop firmly grasped in her right hand again. The tab was a wide loop of leather. She slapped it down hard on the piano lid, making a sound like splintering timber. The piano strings reverberated in sympathy.

'I've waited long enough,' she barked. 'Hold out your left hand, Natasha. This is mere stubbornness on your part.'

'Evelyn, no!' Natasha protested, totally bewildered at what was happening to her. 'You know this is just desire for revenge on your part. You're abusing your position.'

'Hold out your hand, girl,' the woman insisted viciously. 'You know nothing of what my position is here.'

Before Natasha could decide what to do next, Evelyn grabbed her arm and forced it down onto the piano top. Natasha remembered how easily she dominated her when they were last together in Astrid's office, and knew resistance would only be futile and make her appear ridiculous. Looking up, she saw Evelyn's menacingly raised arm and the crop above her head. The scarlet leather tab quivered in the air, ready to strike.

'You will take six for poor preparation and another six for insolence,' the woman decreed. 'Are you ready?'

With great reluctance, and once again finding it impossible to defy the woman, Natasha raised her hand and held it out with the palm upward. There was a terrible pause, during which the glee felt by Chloe hit Natasha almost tangibly, and then the crop hissed down through the air to land across the cushion of her thumb. It was just a ranging shot. Evelyn quickly grabbed Natasha's wrist to hold it steady as she delivered three more assaults in rapid succession, striking the middle of her fingers with tear-inducing effect. Natasha pulled free with a gasp, looking at Evelyn in pure horror. Already she could feel the blood throbbing through her fingers.

'You may now present the other hand,' Evelyn ordered severely.

This time the scarlet leather made its impression on her palm, forcing her to cringe away and instinctively put her hand under her arm in a futile attempt to ease the searing pain. 'Please, Evelyn,' she wailed, trying to blink away the glistening tears that blurred her vision, 'that's enough. You've made your point.'

She turned to go, but Evelyn was quick and struck with the speed of a snake, snatching Natasha's ear between finger and thumb. One of the watching girls sniggered, and Natasha sensed an evil anticipation in the air. She protested desperately, but her raven-haired tormentor was too determined and deriving too much pleasure from the situation to relent now. Holding Natasha at arm's length and pulling her head down so that she was in a crouch position, bending from the waist, Evelyn began to mete out an even harsher punishment. Through the thin satin of her dress Natasha received six searing strokes across her unprotected buttocks, the force of the punishment making her jerk in the woman's grasp, the pain making her yelp each time the crop cut into her flesh.

At last her ear was released and there was a burst of catcalls from Chloe and her set. Evelyn stood with hands on her hips, a smile of triumph unmistakably present on her stern features as she looked towards the avidly watching audience.

'Now you too are my creature, Natasha,' she said in a hushed voice that only the two of them could hear. 'Remember this lesson well, even when you are away from here.'

Natasha left the academy in a cold fury. Leaving a few belongings with Kiki, she boarded a flight to Edinburgh with a return ticket supplied by Gloss. She was hoping to see Rory again, but her attempts to phone him proved unproductive. He must have returned to his parents for the Christmas break. She left a voicemail message with her mobile and the Gloss number as a contact. It was so frustrating not being able to make contact, but then she wasn't entirely sure whether Rory wanted to see her again or not.

So her Christmas passed quietly with a few of her mother's friends. The excitement of going to Paris kept her from feeling low, and yet she wasn't too sure how she would take to living in a foreign land with no true friends or family around her. The future remained bright with possibilities, but with occasional clouds of doubt looming over the horizon.

Chapter 7

Natasha was to meet up with Mila at Kiki's basement flat in Notting Hill. She had spent a couple of nights there, looking through all her stuff, deciding what to take to Paris. Natasha knew from Academy gossip that clothes would not be a problem once she was in Paris. Designers and fashion mags showered the models, especially if they knew the paparazzi were likely to follow them around.

It also gave Natasha a chance to spend a short time together with Kiki. Despite the odd fall-out Natasha still regarded Kiki as her best friend because of her loyalty, and the way she could always see the bright side of a situation. She dearly wished she could come to Paris rather than Mila, who was subject to sudden moods and sulks. Natasha felt that she would really need the support of someone she could trust over the next few months.

But Kiki was all wrapped up in her evening course on computer-aided design. She was putting together a personal website as part of a project, and showcasing her paintings. A new notebook with a heliotrope case stood on the kitchen table, and there seemed to be new items of equipment around that she hadn't seen before. When she arrived Kiki had been determined to show her what she was up to.

'The possibilities are just formidable with having your own website, Tash!' she enthused excitedly. 'Look at this!'

The computer screen was suffused with a bright yellow background, most appropriate for Kiki's sunny disposition, thought Natasha. On a closer inspection it turned out to be a section of Van Gogh's Sunflowers blown up to larger than life-size. This was Kiki's home page, containing a photo of herself, fetchingly dressed in a paint-bespattered smock, with some biography and links to other areas of the website. One was for My Picture Gallery, and another was for Messages, with a direct link to Kiki's email address.

'Of course!' Natasha suddenly shrieked gleefully. 'Kiki, I can send you emails from Paris! Why didn't I think of that before?'

'And if you're feeling in need of a great gas you can visit my website. Once it's up and running, of course.'

'And what will you have on it?'

'You can read my latest news, see my latest painting, and maybe even hear my voice.'

'Your voice? Wow, too much! Are you going to sing a greeting to all your website visitors?'

'God, that's totally naff, Tash.' Kiki wrinkled her pretty nose with distaste. 'No, I might compose a poem to go with each of the paintings. Wait till I get video clips showing me at the easel. What do you think?'

Natasha had to smile at her friend's enthusiasm. 'I think I'm going to miss you terribly,' she said. 'Yeah, I'll visit your website on my computer, providing a ray of sunshine on grey afternoons in Paris when I'm not out working.

'How are you getting on with Semyon, by the way? Maybe you could persuade him to take you to France for a long weekend.'

'Fat chance! We were supposed to go to Venice over Christmas, but at the last moment some deal fell through, or something like that. So we couldn't afford it. Great, so we went over to my sister's and had Christmas lunch in a house full of babies and wet nappies.'

Just then the doorbell rang.

It was Mila, and she seemed determined to make a big impression on her arrival in Paris. Under a fox fur coat she was wearing a daringly low-cut strapless handkerchief top in a Paisley pattern, that revealed a large amount of tummy down to her hipster denims. Natasha gave Kiki a warning look that indicated she should forget any wisecracks.

There was no point in wasting time with

pleasantries. Mila had a taxi waiting and Natasha's bags were packed and ready. Suddenly it hit her that she would soon be far away from Kiki, possibly for several months. She felt devastated at the thought, so she gave her friend a big hug.

'Don't let the buggers get you down, Tash,' Kiki whispered in her ear. 'You've got what it takes, so go for it and don't start worrying yourself sick about what others think. If you need cheering up, give me a call.'

'Okay,' Natasha sniffed. 'And I'll give you my phone number and email address when I know them.'

She grabbed her bags and followed Mila out to the sunken forecourt and up the steps to the pavement where the taxi was waiting.

She didn't feel like talking on the long trip to Heathrow, but Mila was in a vivacious mood. Natasha thought she could guess why, but what she said next gave her a shock nonetheless.

'I feel I've been to your friend's flat before, although I'm sure I've never met her before.'

'Oh?' the declaration unsettled and puzzled Natasha. 'How come? She obviously didn't know you.'

'No, darling,' Mila said theatrically, 'I didn't for a minute imagine she would greet me like an old pal. I was there, if indeed it was the same place, for a fresh supply of snow a few weeks ago.'

'Snow?' Natasha liked what she was hearing less and less. 'Do you mean what I think you mean?'

'Snow, Charlie, Big C, whatever,' Mila said dismissively. 'Anyway, it wasn't her I met, but a guy with a really shifty look. He sounded like the villain out of a Bond movie. Know what I mean?'

Natasha's head spun with the implications of what

she was being told; she just couldn't believe that Kiki could be involved in dealing drugs with Semyon. No, it was impossible. Obviously Mila, the dizzy girl, was mistaken about the flat, and the description that sounded similar to Semyon was merely nothing more than a coincidence. It was ludicrous to even doubt her friend, so she would just put the silly idea out of her mind.

Fortunately there was no delay with the flight, and they were promptly met in Paris by Luc, who, Natasha noticed, had a new car.

As they weaved their way through the heavy traffic out of the airport complex he talked away to Mila, who had commandeered the front passenger seat. From overheard scraps of conversation Natasha learnt that their flat was in Montmartre, which was a nice surprise. She remembered her visit there.

The other news was that they would be sharing with two French models who were only eighteen and nineteen. They were a little turbulentes. Luc, unable to find the right English expression, gave Natasha a meaningful look in the rear-view mirror.

'Boisterous?' she offered.

'Yes, boisterous would be the true word for them,' he confirmed. 'Too many late nights and boyfriends. You know – difficult for us PR's who are supposed to protect them from all that kind of thing.'

Natasha smiled back. Secretly though, she was not sure how they would get on together.

Upon arrival at the top floor flat, though, she was really pleased. Although her room faced in onto a courtyard, it had full-length casement windows with a small balcony. Natasha could easily imagine sunning herself in the summer.

It was beginning to get dark, so Luc left them to unpack and settle in.

He was back by nine-thirty the next morning to take them to meet Mme Sommet, the lady in charge of Gloss's new Paris office. Their two flatmates had come back from a night out at around three in the morning, and were still sound asleep.

Luc sighed in despair. 'They will need to change their habits very soon,' he said, shaking his head ruefully. 'The main catwalk shows begin in two weeks and they will have to be ready to work around the clock.'

The two British girls were soon to learn what that entailed as they settled in to life in a new city. Mme Sommet, fearsome in tinted glasses and a matching pearl-grey twin-set, outlined the initial bookings that she had already set up. She worked from a small office on the left bank, with a common stairway not unlike the flat in Montmartre.

Usually the Italian fashion houses brought over their own girls, but this year, Mme Sommet explained in halting English, they were looking for some girls with more mature figures. She had heard this on the grapevine and Gloss had been given first call.

Mila was booked first with Dolce & Gabbana, then with Chi and Volpe, all in the space of a week, and the last two had expressed interest in seeing Natasha's book. Strega had already booked her for their formalwear collection. These shows were still a few weeks away, but in the meantime it was important for the girls to be seen at the right parties where they might possibly be spotted. And this was where Luc came in, with his bulging contacts book.

The girls would also be expected to attend French classes on at least three mornings a week. Once again they would be in Luc's hands, Mme Sommet explained, and he gave his shy grin that was beginning to endear him to Natasha. He would take them around and ensure they got to know the main landmarks of this city of dreams. In the afternoon, by common consent, they went to the Eiffel Tower and had dinner looking down on the lights of the city and the big ferris wheels along the Champs Elysées to the Arc de Triomphe. Then a drive along beside the Seine, with Nôtre Dame lit up like a jewel in the darkness.

Returning to the flat was a dose of reality. Opening the front door, accompanied by Luc who had a key, they were met by a barrage of sound. They were unable to make themselves heard, so Luc strode down the hall to investigate. Just as he did so a tall girl, her striking auburn hair festooned with curlers, walked out into the hall.

She was wearing nothing but a pair of cotton hipster briefs, bright mandarin. Her attention was devoted to fixing her hair, so she nearly collided with Mila and Natasha. She shrieked and her hands went instinctively to cover her small breasts.

Luc whirled around at the sound and was just in time to see a smaller girl with a dark helmet of hair come running out of another room in a towel. She stopped in surprise only inches from him as he retraced his steps. He made an impatient gesture and she disappeared back into the room she had emerged from. The music volume dropped suddenly.

Luc, taking the first girl by the arm, was talking very fast to her. Natasha could tell he was far from pleased, and she and Mila exchanged quizzical glances. The girl was also shooting looks in their direction, uneasy at being caught in such a disadvantageous situation, but Luc would not release her until she had nodded truculently in reply to his insistent questioning.

Still he held her arm as he performed strained introductions, this time in English. Giselle clearly spoke very little and was anyway in no mood to chat. The smaller girl introduced herself as Annie, and spoke English almost flawlessly.

She confirmed that they were about to go out for dinner and then had planned to go to a nightclub. But Luc thought they should come back to the flat after eating and keep the two British girls entertained. Only after this had been agreed did Luc let Giselle go. He reached out and hooked a finger under her knicker elastic, for a moment hindering her further. The look she shot him was like that of a vixen defending her cubs.

In fact, the evening went okay as Giselle and Annie had had plenty to drink by the time they returned from their meal and had loosened up. With a map spread out on the kitchen table they gave Natasha and Mila ideas on places to visit. Annie was a native of Paris and had taken Giselle on a tour of her city when she'd first arrived six months before.

Annie was immediately likeable, but it was Giselle who had been setting the catwalks ablaze and was imminently to appear on the front cover of style bible Prédictions. If Annie felt any envy she didn't show it. She had trained to be a teacher and intended to become one in due course, but her career plans changed when she was spotted by a talent scout on the beach at Cannes.

Soon the talk turned to the one person they all had in common, and Mila was the one to ask.

'So, how did lover boy Luc get into this line of business?'

Annie translated to Giselle, who rolled her eyes heavenwards. She looked stunning in just a black camisole and skirt, her flame-coloured hair up.

'He used to have a boutique, how do you say?' Annie said.

'We say boutique too,' Natasha confirmed.

'But it went pouf,' Annie went on, in her rich French accent. 'I think his partner was responsible. She was also his girlfriend. And she ran off with someone else. So now he goes into the PR business and I think he still has some mauvais sentiments against us women.'

'You mean, because he is so strict about late nights and boyfriends he bears a kind of grudge?' Mila asked.

Annie nodded. 'Yes, that and other things, which I think you will discover soon enough.'

'Is he good at his job though?'

'Bien sur! He knows people in all the major fashion houses. He has ordered from them all and knows the way they operate. But he must also find out the best parties and night-clubs. For that he is a little too old, I think I must say.'

'Oui, trop trop ancien,' agreed Giselle, who had been listening intently.

'He thinks the parties we go to are just to take drugs,' said Annie. 'It's partly true, of course, but unlike some of the PR's, he will not supply cocaine.'

Mila looked crestfallen. 'So how do you find your supplies?' she asked, and Natasha sensed an urgency in Mila's question. Luckily for Mila, with Annie as reluctant translator she found out where Giselle sourced her requirement. Just down the hill around the cafés on the Pigalle was one of the busiest places for dealers. Normally she phoned for home delivery, which could be risky if the marchand was being followed by the police.

Natasha was determined to stay clear of cocaine, knowing how prevalent coke and crack taking were amongst some of the girls. Much of her time during the first few weeks was taken up with the French classes where she joined others, mainly American students, in a converted mansion only a few blocks away. The classes finished in mid-afternoon, leaving her free to do her own thing or, occasionally, to undertake Gloss commissions.

She had taken the metro one afternoon after class to Opéra, and had come up into the grande place to be confronted by the gilded splendour of the opera house emerging from a mass of scaffolding like a chrysalis turning into a butterfly. She made her way to the Galeries Lafayette, where she was supposed to be taking part in a Buy British campaign the following week. Mme Sommet had told them Natasha's French would be good enough to allow her to hand out samples of food or freebie souvenirs.

The briefing with the manageress went well. Natasha understood most of what she said and was able to ask intelligent questions. She then spent time wandering through the huge store, admiring both the merchandise and the extraordinary art nouveau interior decoration.

Natasha emerged into the pale autumn sunset and wondered if she would be brave enough to order a pressé on her own. She looked through the glass into the warm interior of a café on a side street off the Avenue de l'Opéra, and decided it was time to risk it.

She took a seat close to the window and informed the attentive waiter of her order, without consulting the menu, which she knew might tempt her into something extremely high calorie. During her two weeks in Paris she'd had precious little time to herself. Annie had been very good at taking them around the city when she had free afternoons, and one weekend they went to visit her father who lived at St Denis on the northern outskirts.

Now Natasha had some time on her own she began thinking of home, particularly of Edinburgh. Although she had phoned her mother and Kiki a few times she still hadn't dared to call Rory. Why hadn't he tried to get hold of her through the Gloss London office number she had left? She had to face it, he obviously wasn't that interested in her any more.

'Natasha, what are you doing here? I thought it couldn't be you.'

So engrossed was she in her thoughts she had failed to spot the figure of Luc in a group of men over at the bar. The rest were now leaving, calling farewells to the patron. Luc sat down opposite her and swivelled round with his back to the window, as if the view were the last thing he wished to see. He was wearing the same soft leather jacket as usual, but this time with a burgundy silk scarf and casual trousers. He looked across at her with a darting smile.

'So, you are looking very well,' he said. 'What are you doing here? Waiting for someone important?'

She shook her head, and said, 'No, I've just been for an audition. Were those your friends you were with?'

'In a way,' he mused. 'They are colleagues. We all work for the agencies, helping to promote the models. The kind of work I do for you, Natasha, and for your friend, Mila.'

'She's not exactly a friend. More of a colleague'

Natasha stopped, realising she had echoed him, and they both laughed. He asked if she wanted another coffee, and she compromised with a diet cola.

He came back with the drinks and they fell into

talking quite naturally. Luc's English was uneven but easily understandable. Natasha checked the instinct to correct him. Then she told him about the French classes.

'So why don't you take some lessons with me?' he asked. 'I am an excellent teacher.'

She smiled at this assumption on his part. But he was perfectly serious, and, he added, possibly she could advance his English for him.

'So where do you live, Luc?'

'Just around the corner. I have a big apartment and one day I might louer one room, how do you say it?'

'Let it out to someone?'

'D'accord, exactly. But there is a problem in finding the right sort of person. And is it to be man or woman, I ask myself?'

She couldn't help smiling.

'Would you like to visit?' he asked. 'It has an elevator, unlike yours.'

Natasha hesitated only a second before agreeing. She wasn't entirely sure whether he meant right away or at some time in the future. She decided to leave that to fate. He finished his coffee and indicated he was ready to go.

Looking back on that first time they made love she was surprised at how forward she was in leading Luc on. Initially things took an unusual turn; Luc seemed interested only in kissing when they entered the top-floor flat. She was the one who began to undress him. She felt for almost the first time how it was to be in control.

He lay naked on the bed and watched her as she did a slow strip by the draped balcony window. Then, wearing only a pair of pants and matching lilac leg-warmers she stood astride him on the bed. Amazed at her own self-confidence, she knelt over him, her legs astride his hips. Then she took his swelling weapon in her hand and gently cajoled it to a state of readiness. The veins stood out angrily as she moved its inflamed tip towards her lips.

She felt his whole body tense as her mouth circled its ribbed contours and pushed softly downwards, tightening her lips to increase the pressure. She teased at his manhood's hardness with tongue and teeth, hearing his breathing come harsher and faster. The salt taste of the member's early weeping was on her tongue. She took its length and circled its stiffness in her fist, her thumb and fingertips barely meeting.

She began to pump Luc's weapon into a final state of readiness, watching his face carefully for signs that his climax was approaching. But suddenly he reached out to remove her hand.

'No, I do not want it like this,' he whispered huskily. 'I want you to have pleasure. I am not a poupée.'

He slid out from under her and pushed Natasha onto her back, holding her there with a hand on her chest and probing her sex through the thin fabric of her underwear. She was already aroused to the point where her sex lips were slippery with her secretions. She squirmed and gasped and held his wrist for a moment. But the intensity of the pleasure was too much and she let him have his way. She arched her back and he slipped the pants down her thighs. He removed them and the leg warmers with a single flourish. Both were now naked. She was on the verge of her first Parisian affair.

Natasha felt Luc caress her body with a liquid touch. At the same time he was moaning softly under his breath. She reached for his rod, and to her surprise found it soft again. He pushed her hand away and began to tweak her nipples between the ball of his thumb and the edge of his teeth. She gave a cry from the back of her throat at the intensity of sensation. He was tapping into the whole nervous system of her body spread out under him. She was on fire with impatience. Inevitably, as his lips moved further down, the waves of pleasure increased.

Now Luc was taking her vulva between his lips and pinching its slippery folds. She moaned with pleasure, reaching down to run her fingers through his hair. A hand was cradling her buttock, kneading and stroking as he once again moaned under his breath. Through the mists of her delight Natasha tried to clear her mind sufficiently to make out what he was saying.

With a shock she felt his fingertip stroking right into the cleft of her buttocks, reaching down to her other secret entrance. She squirmed and tensed, unsure of whether she wanted this from him. But his finger continued to probe further, seeking the true entry point of her vulnerability. The sensation at the very ring of her anus confirmed that his fingertip was entering her. Putting shame aside, she gave in and let him master her as the wave of pleasure threatened to engulf her.

Afterwards as they lay side by side, she asked why he didn't come to an orgasm too. Luc mentioned his partner and told the story more or less as she had heard it from Annie. Just as their small chain of boutiques was at last making money, she withdrew most of the money in their business account and ran off with a male model. Legally there was little he could do, but it was the betrayal that hurt most of all. Natasha sensed it in his voice as he told her, gazing at the ceiling and smoking.

She didn't like to ask him just what the words were that he moaned while bringing her to the crest of orgasm. It sounded like, 'Tu acquitteras cela. Tu l'acquitteras.'

It meant little to Natasha. But as the days passed she and Luc became closer and the same pattern developed in their lovemaking. He never penetrated her, and always intoned this same mantra as he brought her to climax.

As the Buy British week began he would drop into the Galeries to say hello and take her for a coffee during time off. Then, when her day was finished, they would go back to his flat and Luc would usually cook. The other benefit was that he had a computer and she was able to visit Kiki's website and see her latest paintings. She also phoned her whenever she needed cheering up. By the time the new autumn shows began Natasha had a key to the apartment, even though she would return to her bed-sit in Montmartre, usually in the early morning by taxi.

Mila was curious to know where Natasha spent her time. Because of her lack of French she was getting less work opportunities on the promotions side, but her supply of photographic work was regular. Mme Sommet was starting to pressurise her into improving her French and the girls in the flat did what they could to get her to speak it. But she didn't have much confidence in her ability to communicate, and most of the photographers had reasonable English, anyway.

At times Mila was very depressed, and then she was just as suddenly on the crest of a wave. Her cocaine habit was now even more pronounced. She didn't even try to hide it at the catwalk shows. Giselle, who was away in Antibes for a magazine shoot, had set her up with a dealer. There would be a ring on the intercom, and Mila would be waiting ready to release the street door.

One evening, after another show was over, Luc invited Annie and Mila to accompany Natasha and him to a night spot in the African quarter. They went past one of the moulins, with its sails in a cross shape. High above them towered the huge white dome of Sacré Coeur, lit brilliantly against the sky. Then Luc turned suddenly down a steep side street that brought them to a small restaurant with green shutters, its sign proudly proclaiming Le Marrakechois. Annie and Mila jumped out excitedly and went to read the menu chalked up on a blackboard by the entrance.

'Couscous with everything!' Annie exclaimed. 'But the music is good.'

Luc seemed preoccupied, Natasha thought. Earlier he had hung around in the background when all the hugs and kisses were being exchanged and the show's designer was being fêted by the fashion press. It was he who had suggested they cut out the usual canapés and champagne reception afterwards. Now they were here he shook hands with a man in a fez who Natasha took to be the proprietor.

They talked in animated French before they were taken to their table at the far end, which had a small raised stage. Luc revealed that there was to be a floorshow later on. And sure enough, as they were being served thick coffee, the lights dimmed and recorded dance music blared.

A girl in a short veil, festooned in trinkets and wearing a traditional green and flame-coloured muslin skirt, stepped onto the stage. Around her hips was a gold knotted sash. This was the first time Natasha had seen the belly dance performed in the flesh. The diners, many of whom must have been from north Africa, watched intently as the girl began to flick her hips in time to the syncopation of the music.

Her dark eyes flashed above the veil, adding to the sensuality of her bodily grace, only glimpsed through gossamer layers. The watchers leaned forward, their look intent. The girl tore aside the veil as the music reached a crescendo and, coming down from the stage, tossed it to one of the diners, who held it up to his lips. She came back to deafening applause.

'This is the patron's son who performs next,' Luc leant over to whisper in her ear, and she caught the familiar acrid scent of the gitanes he was smoking. 'He wants to go into modelling. Tell me what you think.'

A tall, slender boy with fine dark eyes and a mass of dark curly hair and long bushy sideburns took the microphone and did a few dance steps as he waited for the introduction to his song to complete. He was wearing a lilac shirt with a ruffed front and a gold necklace. Natasha was put off by his flashy style, but when she heard his voice she was prepared to forgive him any errors of taste, however large.

It was a heart-rending love song and he gave it a full-throated performance that was exciting to watch and to hear. The audience was on its feet at the end. And the proud patron came and put his arm around the broad shoulders of his son. He was called Hassan. After he had talked with some of the diners, he was brought over to their table. Mila made room beside her.

The youth only spoke French, so Natasha struggled a little and depended on Luc to provide a translation. The upshot seemed to be that Hassan was studying economics at the Arab Institute, but he wanted to earn some extra income modelling. Luc seemed disposed to help the boy and they each drank the other's health in brandy.

After an hour or so of this Luc was becoming loud and effusive, and when they rose to leave he could hardly stand. There was nothing for it; Natasha would have to drive him home.

Luckily by now Natasha had memorised the route from the times she had been back and forth with Luc. The two girls said goodnight, clearly relieved to get away, and headed back to the flat. Natasha said she would get a taxi over later. By now it was well after midnight and the air outside was sharp.

Luc insisted Hassan come with them to have a night-cap, and the boy, not wanting to fall out with the man who could help his modelling career, agreed to come along. Natasha wasn't too happy, but decided not to have an argument with Luc on the pavement.

Somehow she managed to find a parking space close to Luc's flat and she and Hassan got him into the elevator, a cigarette dangling from his lips. Once back on familiar turf Luc became more coherent and insisted on opening a bottle of pastis. The two of them settled down on the sofa, while Natasha went over and warmed herself by the gas fire. Soon they were talking in slurred French that she found impossible to follow.

She asked Luc to tell her what they were saying, though what she really wanted to do was call a taxi and leave. Luc staggered over and put his hands on her shoulders. His gaze was still unfocused but he was able to speak his usual brand of English.

'I was saying to Hassan that he must watch out for male models who are faggots, how do you say it, strange?'

'Queer?'

'Yes, d'accord. There is a danger there for a young boy. But he says to me there is no danger. He is a man who only is attracted by women. Very good, I say. Then I ask him to prove it.'

'Luc, whatever do you mean?'

'I ask him to show me that he is attracted to you. After all, you are beautiful and he is only a little younger than you.'

He put an arm around her shoulders, but she recoiled.

'I still don't see what you mean,' she said slowly. 'Is this to be for you to watch?'

His eyes narrowed and he gave a parody of that shy smile as he ran one hand through his hair. Then something caught his eye and Natasha turned to follow his gaze. Hassan had stood and was removing his shirt, to reveal a well-moulded torso, his skin the colour of café au lait and without any hair. Then, with a quick enquiring turn of his head to check with Luc, he undid the silver buckle of his belt and sat back on the couch to remove his trousers. He wore a pair of lilac briefs that scarcely held in check a male bulge of magnificent proportions.

Natasha was transfixed by the sheer animal beauty of his physique, and her eyes roamed freely. She had never been so close to coloured flesh, and suddenly she was aware her senses were super-sensitive to every move he made. He caught her gaze and smiled arrogantly, preening himself as if in a mirror. Then with a flourish he pulled down the briefs to reveal genitals that were evidently a source of immense pride. A curly fringe topped a rigid stalk, which pulsed with intent as it lay back against his lower belly.

Hassan reached down to cup his own maleness. Natasha could not tear her eyes away. Even as she looked, nature took its course and the rod heaved upwards in his fist, the gnarled veins standing out vividly, and her stomach knotted as if in a gentle reminder to her of her womanhood.

'Natasha, chérie, he wants you,' Luc urged in hushed tones. 'I am asking you to go to him.'

Inexplicably, as if in a dream, she simply could not deny either of the two intense men.

'Déshabillez-vous, mademoiselle, s'il vous plâit,' Hassan croaked.

Natasha reached to the zipper of her dress and slowly pulled off the garment. She stood only in a slip and a pair of textured rouge hold-ups. She was about to ease the slip over her head, when Hassan waved a finger and reached to take her in his arms. She caught the full scent of his maleness and, as they closed together, was aware of his erection probing through the thin rayon slip. His dark eyes were glazed with desire. She knew her pussy was wet for him, and was in no doubt what Luc was expecting of her now, and couldn't believe that she was prepared to fuck the youth just for Luc's amusement.

Hassan turned her round so that she was facing Luc, who was now slumped in a chair, his eyes narrowing as he drew fitfully on a cigarette. Hassan was behind her, breathing fast, his hands coming round to ease down the shoulder straps of her slip until her breasts were finally bared. She was displayed for Luc's pleasure. Luc was aroused, leaning forward and watching intently as Hassan played with her breasts, his strong brown hands pushing them upwards to make the nipples stiffen in response.

She felt his rigid column of flesh brush her buttocks and her breath came faster. She could not resist as the slip was being eased up over her hips. His other hand snaked round to take her vulva between thumb and forefinger, spreading its seeping liquor back and up as his fingers slid the full length of her cleft. Hassan was murmuring endearments in her ear, or were they softly spoken obscenities? She no longer cared.

Releasing her breasts, he pulled the shift firmly up and over her head and threw it to Luc, who was sitting with his hand at his lap.

'Faîtes des progrès, camarade!' he rasped.

Natasha felt herself being bent towards the floor as Hassan pushed her firmly down into a crouch. Then he held her by the hair and pulled to indicate that she should arch her back and present her hindquarters. There was now a greater sense of urgency in his actions. His other hand snaked between her thighs and guided her pubic mound so that he could ease into her. She almost swooned as her sex lips were prised apart by his large cock. Then Natasha felt her vagina respond in a series of warm contractions that slowed his male presumption of easy entry.

The young Moroccan hissed in a mixture of impatience and pleasure. He obviously expected his sexual partner to be compliant, but she would resist as long as she felt able. She felt him increase the frequency of his thrusts, sensing that soon she would be totally compliant to his will. Looking back between her legs she could see his bloated balls restricted in a tight scrotum, but still slapping against her clit. It was an intensity of physical sensation she had never previously experienced. Its brutal force made Natasha feel the inappropriateness of any remaining shreds of shame. Her groans become louder, animal cries of release forced from the depths of her own womanhood.

Then a hand pulled her head up by the chin. She was facing Luc's erect penis, a mere minnow by comparison with the Moroccan's. But she felt a sense of familiarity as she enclosed its head with her lips and took its length. Within seconds Luc had come, doubled up with the spasms of his release. But that was soon out of her consciousness. She was hardly aware of it, the glowing fire of sex within her now spreading inexorably. It was percolating through every fibre to her very extremities. Still she resisted succumbing completely. When she let go she knew she would plunge from the precipice of her pleasure into the pool of ecstasy.

Hassan grasped her shoulders and pulled her almost upright. Looking down, Natasha could see his penis pumping into her with machine-like regularity. His deep cries reverberated through her, reminding her of the husky beauty of his voice. Then with a massive groan he pulled out and suddenly she was empty. He pushed her down and turned her onto her back, and the hot jets of his sperm arced down onto her heaving breasts and her throat. Luc clapped and whistled in a mock, drunken applause.

It had been overpowering, but now she felt empty, rejected, whimpering pitifully as she reached down to finish her own orgasm. This was something she owed herself. Then, when she was through, she hurriedly dressed and left the flat without a further word.

A week later there was one of the last catwalk shows of the season, at the Ritz. It was probably the most high profile of them all, a sensational autumn/winter preview. The incident with the Moroccan had upset Natasha badly and she hadn't answered Luc's calls for several days. Eventually he had come round and asked if Natasha could keep an eye on the flat while he was away for a few days. The shy smile now seemed grotesque.

Why couldn't he grow up? Natasha began to understand why the former partner had left him, and found it difficult to be sympathetic. She allowed him a civil peck on the cheek, but he didn't refer to the incident. Natasha also knew he had been out at night-clubs, chaperoning other models.

Whatever the reason, when the Ritz show arrived Natasha felt lacklustre and depressed. It was then that Mila, who knew most of what had been going on with her and Luc, offered her a snort. Just a sensation, as she put it, to set Natasha up for the next couple of hours. And sure enough, her mood was transformed. She felt as if she were pulsing with new energy, and her smile would surely blind with its dazzle.

As she went out for her final bow with the other girls in the outfit she loved best, a mini-length white party dress with no back and ruching down one side, Natasha felt supremely alive. The audience was on its feet and the flash-guns were like prolonged lightning.

But this use of cocaine must be the first and the last time, she told herself.

Never again.

Natasha's dark Slavic looks had ensured her a busy season. But, as Gloss filled her diary and gladly took their enhanced commission, the demands of appearing almost every day in front of the camera or a critical crowd were taking their toll. She began to dread each day and feel panicky when anything went slightly wrong with the arrangements. She took to arriving far too early for rehearsals and spent hours worrying herself sick. But she was now earning money that she would not have dreamed of a few months before. Any night of the week she could be in the best night-clubs with a choice of men. Paris was being good to her; she would be crazy to throw in the towel now.

Some evenings Natasha couldn't stand being cooped up in the Montmartre flat, and as glorious spring at last arrived she would spend her free evenings in the bars and cafés of the Boulevard de Clichy, watching the prostitutes and pimps at work on the pavements outside. She felt the need to escape from the world of ostentation and hype.

Natasha was always amazed at how blatant the working girls were in displaying themselves, many wearing only underwear and a short fur jacket. They would come into the café when trade was slack and the weather had turned cold or wet. She would smile at them and they would exchange a few commonplace remarks, but she usually found them difficult to understand.

One night she and Mila were at a table near the window, and Mila was being uncommunicative and edgy. Suddenly she got to her feet to attract the attention of an Algerian in a sharp suit who had just come in. Natasha was amazed at how confident Mila's French suddenly became when she had to negotiate with a dealer. And clearly she was a valued customer. The transaction was completed, and the man looked expectantly at Natasha.

Looking back, Natasha realised that was probably the point at which she recognised that she was becoming dependent on cocaine. Up to that point she had depended on the generosity of others, mainly lifestyle users, but why shouldn't she be extra sure of her supplies by buying some for herself? She could well afford it, after all. She may even have persuaded herself it was to pay back the girls she had cadged off. Whatever the reason, she bought one hundred grammes.

Once he'd left they both went to the cloakroom. They were about to leave when they bumped into two girls coming in. They were carrying bright pink and orange holdalls over their shoulders, and Natasha assumed they were strippers between sets.

'Sorry, I mean, pardon,' one of them said.

Natasha, gratified at being taken for French, smiled. 'You're Australian, aren't you?' she asked.

'New Zealand, actually,' the same one corrected. 'From Wellington. And you?'

'I'm Scottish, from Edinburgh. And my friend lives in the south of England. We model.'

'I knew it. Soon as I spotted you, I whispered to Frances that you were in the glamour business! I'm Jill, by the way.'

Jill, a long-haired blonde, shook hands with them. And Frances, slightly shorter with her hair cut in a bob, gave them a friendly smile. Both girls were wearing shorts that revealed tanned, athletic legs.

'Have you got a moment?' Jill asked. 'We've only been here around a week and we thought we'd meet up with someone who could show us the ropes. But so far all we've met are creeps.'

'This is prime creep territory,' Mila sneered, curling her lip in distaste. 'Why don't we all have a drink then, and you tell us what you've been up to?'

They all gathered around a bottle of champagne that Mila insisted on buying. Jill and Frances were working a few blocks along the boulevard at the Club 69, a striptease and peepshow joint. Twice a week they had special catfight nights where pairs of girls would wrestle together, usually covered in oil.

'They were looking for girls to do this stuff and, well, we were perfectly qualified, I suppose,' said Frances.

'You mean, you'd done this kind of thing before in Wellington?' asked Natasha.

'Shit no!' Jill snorted. 'We're a pair of fine country girls. No, we both did wrestling at school and we got fairly good at it, didn't we, Frances?'

The dark girl had taken off her top and Natasha noticed that her arms were well toned. She was quieter than the blonde, but Natasha felt she didn't miss much.

'I've never seen women wrestling. What do you wear? How many rounds do you have to do?'

'Well, Natasha, we usually end up wearing very little, if the truth be told. And we don't bother much with rounds; we just stop for a breather every now and then. The noise is usually deafening in there, and these Frenchies just go on shouting. All a bit crazy really, since we agree who's going to win beforehand.'

Frances unzipped her bag and produced a matching set of lycra bra top and hot pants in a jarring colour mix of orange and flame yellow. A large white number nine had been crudely stitched on the top.

'These are what we have to wear,' she said. 'The first time we wore leotards, but Gaston, the boss, told us they were not popular with the customers. Jeez, what creeps! The baby oil ruins them anyway, so he agreed to supply us with the costumes.'

Natasha took the bra and shorts and held them up for inspection, but she realised a group of men drinking at the bar were taking a keen interest, and handed them back to Frances quickly.

'Why didn't the customers like leotards?' she asked. 'Surely they would have been more revealing than this workout stuff. Although I can see it's very eye-catching.'

'Natasha, the truth is we don't wear the costumes for very long. We normally end up in just our pants, and sometimes not even them. Jill likes ripping mine off, but I usually get my own back.'

'Yeah, you're a dirty fighter when your back's on the mat, girl,' Jill grinned.

Natasha sensed the bond between the two young women was strong, and she wondered if it was sexual.

'Hey, why don't you two come along?' Jill suddenly asked. 'It starts at nine, and there's another session at ten. And you won't be the only females there, I can guarantee. There seems to be a special area for women and their escorts.'

After the New Zealand girls left Mila looked at Natasha, bright-eyed. 'Are we going to? I'm up for it,' she giggled.

'But Mila, how about if it's all men in grubby raincoats? I couldn't stand the idea of sitting there with someone in the row behind jerking off.'

Mila pulled a disgruntled face. 'I know what you mean. I stripped in Soho for a couple of weeks, and you know what got to me? It was usually so deathly quiet, and sort of a relief when a rugby crowd arrived one night. That's what got me on to crack in the first place, did I tell you that?'

For a moment the smiling mask dropped from Mila's face and Natasha saw how insecure and frightened she was. She reached over and gave her a hug, feeling the first sobs shaking her frame and the tears smudging on her cheek, and she felt bad about how she had judged Mila in the past. But within a minute or so she was over it, and she looked bright again.

'One more visit to the loo, I think, to renew my friendship with Mr C,' she sniffed, wiping her eyes with the back of a hand. 'Then how about going to see the lady wrestlers?'

Club 69 was an old cinema with a sloping floor and an apron stage created in front of the screen. It was surprisingly opulent inside, or maybe it was just effective use of coloured lights that bathed everything in a purple glow, except for the brightly lit stage, which had a thick rope surround at about waste height.

Natasha asked for Gaston and, to her surprise, they were shown to seats next to the stage right at the front, and offered complementary drinks. She guessed that Jill must have spun him a good tale about how their guests were famous models.

A stripper was just finishing her act, and as their eyes adjusted to the low lighting the girls were able to see that the women in the audience and their escorts were restricted to either side of the stage. Since these areas were raised they had a good view of what was going on. When the stripper had completed her act, which involved doing the splits can-can style between two chairs, there was a round of applause and the stage lights faded.

Then there was an announcement about a 'spectacle uniquement erotique et sensationelle', involving 'deux jeunes specialistes du catfight'. A buzz went round the club, nowhere more than in the female-only enclosures. Two well-endowed young men were busy laying a padded mat, then a bright blue tarpaulin across the stage, securing it with cleats at the corner posts but leaving the middle section dipping below the ropes.

Then, without delay, a fanfare played over the sound system. The black curtain at the rear of the stage twitched apart to allow four figures to emerge. Then the stage was bathed in light again and Jill and Frances, resplendent in their pink and yellow kits, dipped into the ring as the rope was held up by the two young attendants, now dressed only in trunks and bow-tie.

'Mesdames et messieurs, faites bon accueil s'il vous plaît aux Filles de Wellington!'

Another blast of fanfare music as the two New Zealand girls limbered up, staking out a corner each. Frances looked over her shoulder and Natasha waved to attract her attention, but she seemed blinded by the spotlights. In the far corner Jill tossed her blonde tresses before putting her hair up in a scrunch. Then, with no referee or bell, they closed on each other, Frances going for Jill's long legs, heaving and bringing her down with a gasp on the floor.

In a trice the dark girl was on her, pinning her legs with her hands and placing toned thighs over the other girl's shoulders. Already there were shouts encouraging 'numero six!' or 'numero neuf!' as wagers were made.

Grasping Jill's legs in one arm Frances reached down with the other to tug at Jill's shorts. Suddenly they came, and it was a simple matter despite her protests to slide them up to her ankles. Then gathering her under the knees, Frances moved round to Jill's boob tube with its large white number nine, grabbing it and exposing her breasts.

The crowd went wild, particularly the women nearby, who were already on their feet for a better view. Jill somehow regained the initiative, and taking Frances' wrist, held her in a half-nelson while she pushed her down on her front with one foot and pulled off her shorts. Next she reached down and, because of the girl's struggle to break free, only succeeded in ripping her pants so that they hung from one leg. The crowd erupted.

This was too much for Frances. Escaping from the lock, she was on her feet and grabbing her opponent by the boob tube, which had rolled around her waist, she pulled her up bum first and then slipped the lycra garment over Jill's hips and down her legs with great dexterity, leaving her naked. Then she flung it into the audience.

Applause redoubled as Frances removed her own top, revealing a full bust with dark nipples, and the girls grappled once again. This time Jill found a headlock on her opponent, but left herself open to a feint that had her toppling forward onto the tarpaulin. The naked girls writhed and grappled for the advantage, being underneath one moment and the next unbalancing their opponent to gain the advantage.

Then the two bronzed attendants stepped into the ring and squirted baby oil all over them from above. One of the girls swore as it went in her eye. The men then squatted to ensure that oil was covering them.

Jill broke free and spun Frances round so that she almost slid onto her side. Kneeling behind her, Jill, her hair all loose and oily, slipped her arms under the other girl's and joined her hands behind Frances' neck, forcing her head forward and her arms out to the side. Then, carefully in case she slithered free, she rose to her feet bringing the darker girl with her, gleaming and naked, except for the remains of her pants around one knee. Jill leaned back, pulling her opponent's shoulders back while retaining the pressure on her neck.

'Submit! Submit!' she grunted.

Frances was shouting to be heard above the hubbub. The bout was over, and as a result certain members of the audience were handing over money, and there was some applause, mainly from the women members.

Natasha was astonished to find she was quite excited by the spectacle of two beautiful girls fighting, and she and Mila went to say hello again during the break. Then Natasha had an idea; Luc was still away, so she would invite everyone back to his flat for a drink.

The second bout took place immediately after the intermission and, after showering, the two girls joined them at their table. Gaston came over and handed them their wages, and said something they did not understand, so Natasha managed to interpret for them.

'I think he says he wants you to shout and swear more, to make it more realistic.'

'What, in French?' asked Jill.

'No, you're okay. In English.'

'Okay, mate,' Frances smirked, 'you're in for an earful on Friday night!'

They left and took a taxi to Luc's. The flat was stuffy because she had not been round for a couple of days, and when she tried to light the stove to make coffee she discovered the gas was turned off. Eventually they found the meter, and began to relax.

'Girl, you were fighting pretty serious on that second bout,' said Jill, with a girlish pout.

'Yeah, well that was to get you back for that full-nelson in the first bout. That was really hard. Did you expect me to submit?'

'Actually, I didn't. But I got you in a good

grapevine. You must be getting soft.'

They both giggled and snuggled up to each other. Natasha envied them their easygoing relationship. At least they could trust each other. She was feeling increasingly rootless and disoriented with all the partying and designer tantrums. So far she had met no one she could call a real friend, apart from Luc, who had now destroyed their bond of trust. Maybe a snort of C would lift her mood; it was the third one that evening but desperate measures were needed, she told herself.

The girls talked for an hour or more, joints were passed around, and then the Antipodean girls said they were getting sleepy. They were staying temporarily in a women's hostel, so Natasha invited them to stay at the flat. She knew where Luc kept clean sheets, and he wouldn't be back for another couple of days. They could let themselves out in the morning and she would come by later to tidy up properly after them.

The following morning Natasha was woken by an early phone call. It was Luc, almost speechless with fury. There had been a gas explosion in the bathroom of the flat. He had arrived a few hours afterwards from Toulouse to find extensive water damage and the bathroom a total write-off, and it was only then that he discovered there had been two strange girls staying the night.

Natasha afterwards discovered that it had happened when Jill decided to roll one last joint, sitting on the toilet. The pilot light on the water heater had not ignited when they'd turned on the gas. She was shocked but apparently not burned, and the two of them were in hospital overnight for observation. Natasha felt terrible about it and phoned the hospital, but they had left after breakfast.

The upshot was that Luc blamed the girls for causing the damage and Natasha for letting them stay the night. When she tried to explain about the gas he wouldn't listen. The insurance probably wouldn't pay up, he screamed, since he wasn't occupying the flat. He was through with her, and she had better get ready to pack; he would make sure no agency would take her on in Paris.

And he was as good as his word.

The following Monday Natasha was handed a sealed envelope by a stony-faced Mme Sommet, informing her that she had been letting down the good reputation of Gloss by taking drugs and being photographed at a strip show. She was dismissed as of that week.

Chapter 8

'I want you to know I do appreciate this, Kiki,' Natasha said. 'I'd never have landed on my feet if you hadn't agreed to give me a roof over my head.'

'By the balls of Godzilla, Tash, drop it!' her friend exclaimed. 'You're putting me off something desperate. Here am I trying to get a typical attitude of you, and you're maundering on about being eternally grateful. It just isn't you, kid.' She heaved a mock sigh.

Natasha kept her thoughts to herself and tried to keep still. She had only returned to London a few days before, and her future was still wide open. She felt relieved to be rid of Luc, without a doubt. But there was a disappointment that she had left Paris so quickly, with just some more catwalk shots in her book to show for it.

Natasha now had serious doubts about continuing to model. The balance she had received from Gloss meant there need be no great urgency. She might invest some of it into her textile design business, and she felt her modelling experience, brief as it had been, might give her an inside track.

But she was finding it difficult to get back into creative work. The days just floated by without really achieving anything.

In the months Natasha had been away Kiki finished her website classes. Now she was working from home designing sites for individuals and small businesses. She had been showing Natasha how to make a homepage, and the portrait, which they would later scan in, was to make it distinctive. She might, Kiki told her, be able to sell some textile designs online.

'Do you really think the website could help my designs become better known?' Natasha asked. 'How would the manufacturers and the retailers get to know about it?'

'Well, one way is to send out a leaflet telling the important people that you have one. Or you could advertise in the trade press, I suppose, although that'll probably be a bit pricey.'

'And if they do actually email me, what happens then?'

'Again, it's up to you. If you can arrange a meeting that's probably the best way. You know, meet the buyer and flash your tits at him.' She giggled, and added, 'Even at her, in some instances, I guess. Otherwise you could send an attached file or even a CD-rom with your full catalogue on it and an order form. If you're lucky you might get an order from that old pervy flame of yours.'

'You mean Jim?'

'Who else? So what do you think?'

'Well, I suppose it could be quicker than doing cold calling.'

'Actually, I meant the portrait,' said Kiki, pouting playfully. 'A perceptive study, you must agree.'

She held up the charcoal sketch and Natasha started; her eyes stared back at her as if in shocked recognition. Her face looked gaunt; highly fashionable from a modelling point of view maybe, but she was secretly shaken by the changes. Maybe it had been a mistake to pose with her hair up.

'Yes, I guess so,' she said glumly. 'I do appreciate it, Kiki, but it's always a bit of a shock to see yourself as others see you. Shucks, I can't believe I've actually just said that.

'Will charcoal scan okay into the computer?' she added, trying to forget the disappointment of her image.

'Right as rain,' Kiki said brightly. 'But once it's in memory you can start prettying around with it anyway. So don't worry, girl, I can make you look whichever way you want. I can give you chipmunk cheeks or a nose like a horse!'

The following weeks were a worrying time for Natasha. She soon rediscovered that household bills, which of course she shared with Kiki, ate deeply into her nest egg. Although she was producing some fashion textile designs based on new metallic-look fabrics, she hadn't attempted to market them to a manufacturer. The website would be the answer, she kept telling herself, but she would need a good range of samples to show. She could have tried picking up the odd modelling assignment, but she felt it was a closed chapter with the sort of tales Luc was probably spreading.

Then there was the coke. The more anxious she became the more she was tempted into snorting. She tried not to make it a habit, but Kiki nearly always had some about the flat, or knew where to get it. Sometimes people came round and they would smoke grass or go out to these bizarre clubs that Kiki and her friends frequented.

One was called Pushkin's, a scruffy, bohemian venue with a bar selection that was east European, located in an abandoned church. Founded by a friend of Semyon's, Pushkin's was where Kiki and she could always get their drug of choice. It was usually from expat Russians or Georgians with underworld connections.

Natasha noticed Kiki was uneasy about Semyon. She would hear her talking to him on the phone, half in whispers or behind a closed door. She acknowledged at least that he dealt not just in art but in coke and heroin as well, but that didn't seem to have lessened her feelings for him. He was still the man in her life. But they never seemed to meet any more, and Natasha knew Kiki was upset.

Kiki compensated by doing outrageous things with her lesbian friends, such as Letty, a very large girl with a personality to match, who went in for kaftans.

So it was a heart-stopping moment when, across the sunken dance floor at Pushkin's, Natasha caught a glimpse of Semyon. She wasn't sure to begin with because he was dressed in a sharp Italian jacket with a Nehru collar, but the dark jowls and darting look couldn't be disguised by expensive tailoring.

She nudged Kiki. Semyon was standing over a table of girls of a similar age to their group, handing out cards. There seemed to be a lot of interest. As he completed his task he looked around the room, then noticed Kiki.

It was difficult to make out Semyon's expression in the semi-darkness. He came over during a lull in the music, and he and Kiki kissed. Natasha could see her friend was still smitten. Whatever was his appeal, she asked herself for the umpteenth time?

The cards were to recruit girls for a new escort agency he was targeting at businessmen and cultural visitors from former Soviet bloc countries. Semyon's contacts were never-ending, and they always seemed to have deep pockets. And he promised the girls an impressive basic fee.

He must have realised fairly quickly that the sisterhood was not ideal material for a male-centred escort agency, so he concentrated on Kiki and Natasha.

'Semyon, how will we communicate if they don't have much English?' asked Kiki.

'Don't worry, their English will be good, because they are here to trade. That makes sense, does it not? More importantly, I must teach you how a Russian man expects his companion to behave and what to wear.'

'And... and what happens after the dinner date?' Natasha asked carefully.

He smiled. 'That is entirely up to you girls.'

'Girls?' Kiki echoed. 'You mean, we could both be doing it together, with the one man?'

He shrugged indifferently. 'Or maybe it is two men,' he said. 'It will depend on what the customer wants. In Russia today the customer is the king, if he can pay.'

The two girls looked at each other, then Kiki burst into a fit of hysterical giggles.

'I think that means you are interested, no?' He smiled, with a satisfied glint in his eyes. 'And here is a little something on account, babushka.' He bent down to give Kiki a hug, at the same time slipping a small sachet onto her lap. Her hand closed over it and she gave him a conspiratorial smile.

Two days later Kiki's mobile rang. She was in the bath, so Natasha picked it up and took it through to her. It was Semyon. He had two trade attachés for them for the following Tuesday, when an East-West trade meeting was due to start. They should go to the hotel to meet the two gentlemen – as Semyon insisted on referring to them – after the official banquet was finished. If they played their cards right they could be required for three nights or more.

This information was relayed to Natasha as she sat on the edge of Kiki's bathtub. They should wear short skirts, dress young, and be prepared to pose.

'Yeah, okay Semy, comprendo,' Kiki said into the small mobile. 'The two of us? Let me just check with Tash.'

'Oh Kiki, do you think we should?' Natasha said anxiously, still very unsure about the whole thing. On the other hand, she needed the money – and it was good money. 'It's a bit risky,' she went on. 'What if it turns nasty? You know, if they insist on wanting sex or something?'

'Hear that, Semy?' Kiki said again into the phone. 'We're both nice girls, so we don't want any hassle, okay?'

The two of them did as instructed, turning up at a West End hotel at ten-thirty. Clearly they were expected; the concierge didn't bat an eyelid at their flirty outfits.

In the suite they found a grey-haired man with an eye-patch, who they were told to address as the Mastr. A younger man with a full black beard was also there, acting as interpreter. They never did find out what the conference was all about, but the Mastr had clearly enjoyed a very good dinner. He sprawled in one of the stuffed leather armchairs, his considerable stomach escaping over the top of his loosened sash, a seraphic smile on his sweaty face. An emerald ribbon with medal attached hung over one arm.

Kiki was wearing a short skirt of grey leather with pearl-effect stockings. Natasha had decided on a thigh-length little black dress with a string of colourful Mexican beads. They were about to sit on a plush banquette under an ornately gilded mirror, but something in the younger man's eyes halted them.

'No, don't sit down, ladies,' he said. 'You are not here to relax, but to entertain the Mastr. You understand this?'

The two of them, feeling rather like schoolgirls in the presence of a strict headmaster, blushed a little and remained standing.

'He wishes you to strip to your underclothes – instantly,' the younger man went on. 'Please do not keep him waiting.'

The Mastr looked coldly on them. Natasha was going to remind them that sex was not on the agenda, but feeling somewhat intimidated by the overbearing atmosphere, thought better of it. Kiki wore no bra, just powder-pink hipster briefs with a flower pattern. Natasha was glad she had stuck to a black combination with a bandeau bra, that was less revealing. They stood side by side in their bare feet with the mirror behind them.

The younger man, now in shirtsleeves, approached them with two lengths of thick braided cord in a mix of rich colours. Natasha guessed they were the tiebacks for the full-length tapestry curtains.

'Now you will listen carefully,' he said. 'The Mastr wants to see you tied together. You must be like slaves, in bondage. You understand? Good,' he said, eyeing them nodding meekly, 'then no questions please.'

He made them face each other, then raise their forearms to the vertical and clasp each other's hands. He carefully bound their arms together from the elbow to the wrist, first one then the other. They were drawn close to each other. Natasha caught a scent of perfume mixed with something sharper as she looked her friend in the face. Kiki smiled back encouragingly.

They were both made to lean forward, balancing each other with their arms. Natasha looked over in the mirror and saw them posed like wrestlers. Then she noticed that the Mastr's chair was empty. Looking over her shoulder, she saw the younger man now holding an old-style carpet beater made of cane.

'Now for the arrangements,' he said. 'You are very bad girls. The Mastr is displeased and now he watches your punishment from behind the screen. You make no complaint, but after each stroke you must say, "I do it better next time, my Mastr".'

Kiki's astonished expression nearly made Natasha protest, but Kiki bit her lip and quickly flashed her a warning look.

The bearded secretary took up position behind Kiki. He pulled her panties down a little to the tops of her tensed thighs, and then swished the cane implement through the air experimentally, and Natasha felt Kiki tense in anticipation.

Then, as the first stroke cut through the air and impacted on her vulnerable bottom, Kiki jolted upright, her clasp on Natasha's hand tightening as a reflex. Her eyes widened in shock.

'Say it,' Natasha whispered urgently.

'I do it better next time, my Mastr!' Kiki grunted, her face screwed up with the discomfort of the blow.

Another swish and Kiki tensed again, closing her eyes. Natasha wondered how intense the pain could be. Kiki took four more strokes, the last two almost unbalancing her with their force. She tried to move a hand to her stinging buttocks, but was prevented by the bondage. She swallowed a sob and spoke the apology in a whisper, Natasha trying to comfort her.

The secretary scratched his beard and flexed his arm. A gruff voice came from behind the screen, and he went over for a discussion. He returned and made them swivel round so that this time Natasha was in the same position Kiki had occupied. In the mirror Kiki's haunches showed the raw imprint of the carpet beater above the stretched line of her pink underwear. The younger man threw a curt question over his shoulder, then Natasha felt her panties being swiftly pulled down her smooth legs, and she was made to step out of them.

There was a pause, and in the mirror she saw the secretary take the black panties to the man behind the screen. Then the secretary returned, brandishing the beater once again, and Natasha felt his warm hand on the base of her spine, pushing firmly downwards. He grunted at her slight resistance.

Kiki looked sorrowfully at her with red-rimmed eyes, and whispered, 'Think of the money!'

Natasha wasn't too shocked by the force of the first few strokes. She smiled bravely at Kiki and made the necessary apology to the Mastr. From behind the screen there were noises of a man pleasuring himself. After the third stroke she looked up to see his red face half concealed as he held her knickers to his nose and inhaled. His gaze was fixed on her tingling rump.

'I do it better next time, my Mastr,' she croaked.

The next stroke bit into her reddened bottom and she flinched, grasping onto Kiki in the same way as she had done. Natasha was aware that she was no longer arching her back but tucking it in to make it less of a target. Once again the younger man adjusted her posture, this time reaching between her legs and grasping a pinch of her pubic hair to spitefully emphasise his requirements.

'Keep your position, little lady!' he ordered.

She was tempted to reply, but any riposte was cut short by another vigorous stroke of the carpet beater.

'I do it better next time, my Mastr!' she gasped, heat and pain permeating her poor bottom.

The final blow was delivered, and opening her eyes, she saw he was inspecting with keen interest the results of his efforts. Then she felt a rough hand grasping her right buttock firmly, and saw in the mirror that the Mastr was behind her, naked from the waist down, masturbating with her delicate panties in his fist, wrapped around his erection. The secretary had moved behind Kiki, and she writhed as he was touching her tenderised buttocks.

Then, from the expression on her face and her quickened breathing, Natasha knew the young man was touching her friend even more intimately. Kiki began to gently sway her hips as she succumbed to waves of pleasure. Natasha gave her an anxious look, wondering if she would submit to being fucked.

The secretary was smiling thinly through his beard. Sprouting from his unbuttoned shirt she could see a mass of jet chest hair. But then her thoughts were outrageously wrenched back to her own predicament as she heard the Mastr grunt like a pig and felt him releasing his load of hot cum onto her scolded buttocks. A number of times he grunted and spurted his sticky emission onto her fleshy globes, each spasm with gradually decreasing force. Then she felt him, with a possessive hand, wiping his sperm into her skin with her own soft panties. Then he patted her patronisingly on the head and retired to his bedroom.

Their ordeal was over. The secretary untied their bonds and they were allowed to dress, but although money was handed over, neither of them had their underwear returned.

Natasha and Kiki were told to report back to the hotel two days later, and this time they were asked to prepare a 'girl with girl' performance. To their surprise there was a woman present, about the same age as the Mastr. She sat beside him on the chaise longue, smoking a black Turkish cigarette and staring unblinkingly at the two of them.

They had rehearsed an innocent little show that would take about twenty minutes. Kiki wore a French maid's outfit and Natasha was the sophisticated mistress in a long robe, who enjoyed nit-picking and humiliating maid. The hotel suite was ideal for this scenario, and they had planned it out with as little dialogue as possible, aware that the Mastr would have to receive a translation if it became too sophisticated.

First of all Kiki was seen lackadaisically at work with a feather duster. She yawned and rolled her eyes. Then Natasha picked up some of the ornaments to inspect them for dust, eventually running a finger along the marble mantelpiece and showing her the result. She upbraided her with plenty of flamboyant gestures, and heard a guffaw from the Mastr, so they must have crossed any cultural barriers on humour. The woman, however, was sitting stony-faced throughout.

After a while Natasha had Kiki over her lap to give her a spanking. Then she insisted she strip to her undies and bend over the back of a chair. This time she used the same carpet beater, but she could see that Kiki's rump still bore the traces of the previous encounter, so she decided to go easy on her friend.

At this point the maid was supposed to rebel and fight with her mistress, making her strip too, but getting more and more into the act, Kiki broke free and approached the bearded secretary. He was sitting on a chair to the Mastr's right, where he could whisper any explanations into his ear. Here Kiki did a total strip right in his face, dropping her lacy underwear at his feet. He looked unmoved, as Kiki retreated with a saucy smile.

Then they resumed the show. Natasha was pushed over a table and Kiki unzipped her dress from the back. She pulled it down and dropped it around her ankles. Natasha stood upright, mimicking fury, and grabbed Kiki by the hair. They ended up rolling on the floor together. Then Kiki eventually got on top and pulled down Natasha's bra to expose her breasts. This was something they hadn't actually planned, and it took Natasha by surprise, but she knew they had better make the next few minutes convincing if they were to expect a fee as generous as the last time.

She felt Kiki's warm hands sliding down over shoulders, and the straps of her bra were pulled free of her arms. Then Kiki's head dipped down as her tongue began to play with the nipple of her right breast. She felt the gooseflesh rise and her nipple pushing eagerly upwards like a seed sprouting towards the light. She felt Kiki's soft lips nuzzling like a baby's to encircle the aroused nipple. A sigh escaped her moist lips as she instinctively reached up to stroke Kiki's soft neck and hair, and her free hand cupped her own breast, offering more of it to her friend.

Then Kiki pulled away a fraction and looked her straight in the eye, her expression one of dreamy lust. Natasha suddenly remembered they had kissed passionately once before, when they were very drunk. But now, in the intensity of the moment, it seemed quite natural to be so intimate, and she felt herself responding to her friend. It was a breathlessly close physical union, more relaxed than the fevered coupling with a man.

Their gaze still locked, Kiki reached back, her hand moving slowly down over Natasha's tummy to slip under the waistband of her panties. Oh God, what was she going to do now? This they definitely hadn't rehearsed. Her fingertips stopped enticingly just millimetres short of the cleft of Natasha's sex, her hand concealed under the peach-coloured lace.

'Pretend to come,' Kiki whispered in her ear. 'Make it good.'

Natasha began to raise her hips and moan softly. Kiki lay over her, sucking her erect nipple again. Natasha arched her back, her breathing swift and shallow. She was trying to bring off a convincing performance of a woman in the final throes, but just then Kiki extended two fingers and rubbed delicately at her hooded clit, and all pretence vanished as a throb of exquisite pleasure took Natasha by complete surprise.

This time the groan came from the back of her

throat with no prompting. Kiki's busy fingers worked expertly, and Natasha felt herself begin to melt, only vaguely aware that Kiki was again watching her responses intently, sensitive to every flickering expression of delight and longing.

Natasha lost all sense of time and place. When the moment of sheer ecstasy came she knew it was something different – and wonderfully special. She lay limply beneath the reassuring weight of her friend, her eyes closed, feeling totally relaxed, her body aglow...

Then, with a rush of guilt and shame, she remembered they were being watched. There was a buzz of conversation from nearby. She opened her eyes and rolled her head to the side, and saw the woman staring at her with intent.

When Natasha answered Kiki's mobile the following evening she thought she was suffering from a bad case of wish fulfilment.

'Natasha, is that you?'

Natasha immediately recognised Rory's voice.

'That's extraordinary,' he said, upon hearing her voice. 'I can't believe it. I was given this number by a friend of Kiki's. She said she'd passed on my flat number to her some months ago. That's why I was phoning, to see if Kiki had a contact number for you. I've heard nothing from you for so long. Did you get the messages I left?'

'No, I've been in Paris,' Natasha explained.

'I know. I thought that's where you were right now. I left two messages with Gloss and they said they would pass them on to the Paris office. It was to give you my mobile number. But total silence, so this was my last throw.'

She felt her anger rising at the thought that Rory

had been leaving messages for her that hadn't got through. Then it dawned on her; Luc was in Mme Bonnet's office at least once a week, so what if he had offered to take the messages but deliberately not passed them on?

'So, will I see you again?' she asked hopefully.

'Will next week do?' he said enthusiastically.

'What, here in London?'

'Where else? Are ye glaikit, lassie? I'm coming down for an interview on Thursday.'

Her head spun. It all seemed like a dream. She couldn't think what to say.

'So what are you up to?' he went on. 'Still modelling?'

'No, I had enough of it in Paris. I didn't believe them when they told me it was going to be stressful. Believe me, it is. No, I've gone back to the designing. I suppose I should think of college again, but for the time being I'll stay in London.'

'I should forget college, Natasha,' he advised. 'My final year has been a waste of time, to be honest. Sheer drudgery. I can't wait to find myself a job with an agency. And I've got some contacts lined up, so here goes. Will you be around?'

'Yes, next Thursday, of course. You must come round for dinner.'

Kiki was delighted that Rory had been in touch at last, but she had exciting news of her own. Leonid, the bearded secretary, wanted her to go with him to Geneva where the following week there was to be a major trade exhibition. All she had to do on Friday evening was meet him with her passport and he would have a return ticket for the weekend. She'd be earning incredible money, and they'd be staying in a hotel overlooking the lake. It all sounded wonderful.

But Natasha wasn't so sure. What did they know about either of the two men? And what was the role of the mysterious woman who'd turned up to watch?

Natasha had intended to see her friend off at the airport, but there was a phone call from Leonid to say that an official car would pick her up. They would be able to go straight through diplomatic passport control.

So Natasha waved goodbye from the pavement as Kiki was wafted away in a large black limo with tinted glass. But as she turned to go down the stone steps to the basement flat she felt a sudden chill grip her spine, and a desperate urge to rush back into the road and run after the car.

Why was she feeling so spooked about it? She had, after all, gone off to Paris with no lasting damage done. And Kiki had twice as much savvy as she had.

Natasha had so much work to do on her designs, but she found the weekend dragged abominably, her thoughts preoccupied with both Kiki and Rory. When her mobile rang she assumed it would be Rory to finalise his arrival time, but it was Kiki, and her voice was strangely flat.

'Natasha, I don't have much time,' she said hastily. 'I'm in Geneva, okay? I'll be staying for a few more days, and I probably won't be back in time to see Rory. But don't worry, okay?'

'Are you sure you're okay?' Natasha asked, her unease returning.

'Can't chat, Tash,' Kiki said abruptly. 'It's too expensive, I'll maybe try emailing...'

And then she was cut off. She had spoken faster and faster as if she knew she would be. But surely, Natasha reasoned, the trade delegation could have paid the charges as part of the hotel account. So was it Leonid that cut her off? Had he been right beside her as she phoned?

She was extremely worried, but what could she do? Kiki went of her own accord, and Natasha had nothing to confirm her fears that something untoward was going on. So there was nothing she could say to the police. She must just wait for a few days and hope her imagination was working overtime.

Thursday evening came with no further word from Kiki. By now Natasha's worries had diluted somewhat, convincing herself she'd just been paranoid and that no news was good news. Kiki was probably having a great old time and hadn't even thought about ringing her friend again. And why should she? She wasn't to know Natasha was worrying unnecessarily.

Then suddenly Natasha heard a taxi pulling up outside and, too quickly for her to gather herself, the doorbell rang. There was Rory, just as she remembered him last, standing on the doorstep with a college scarf draped over a tweed coat and jeans.

'Well, am I allowed in?' he grinned.

She rushed around madly, getting him a drink, trying to remember all the news she was going to give him. But her head was all in a whirl. She kept on jumping from one thing to another. Eventually he patted a space on the sofa beside him and, when Natasha sat down, put an arm around her shoulders as if it were the most natural thing in the world.

They talked, and she relaxed. The meal was served eventually, and she had to admit it was a little overdone.

Rory was away at interviews in the morning. They were to meet for lunch before his final one, and then they would have the whole weekend to themselves. He inspected her designs on the Saturday and seemed to be impressed. Natasha showed him the website, even though it was not ready yet. He made a link to his own home page. Then Rory suggested that he might show the designs to a friend who had contacts with a textile mill, if she didn't mind.

'Mind?' she squealed excitedly. 'That would be fantastic. How would you like to become my agent? Do you think we could have a truly businesslike relationship?'

'Worth a try,' he mused. Then his expression became intense. 'Now, what kind of business did you have in mind?' he whispered.

Somehow they never got to visit the Design Museum that weekend, but since the weather was dull they had the perfect excuse to stay in all day and relish the pleasure they gave each other. And they talked and talked. Rory admitted he had fancied her from the moment he saw her in first year. He had even witnessed the incident with the see-through dress in the college garden. He just hadn't had the confidence then to tell her.

The one thing Natasha didn't dare to bring up was the escort work, which turned out to be a mistake. She had gone out to fetch a take-away meal on the Sunday evening while he stayed in to watch a programme he particularly wanted to see. When the phone rang Rory didn't answer it, but the ansaphone was switched on.

As a result he heard Semyon asking if she was free for a booking on Wednesday night. A foreign businessman, he explained in unnecessary detail, who was looking for an intelligent girl interested in the arts. Just perfect for her. A visit to Sadlers Wells was on the cards if she played her cards right, and afterwards, who knows?

So when she returned bearing fried beef and chicken with spring greens, Rory had a face of frost and his bags were almost packed. He played the message to her without a word, and she felt her legs go weak.

He demanded an explanation. In a passion she felt that he should have trusted her to tell him when she felt comfortable about it, and anyway, escort work didn't necessarily mean what he obviously thought it did.

At that Rory retreated into a sullen silence and completed his packing. He was going to spend the night in a hotel and he might phone later when he had calmed down.

That night she cried herself to sleep, and the following morning the cold take-away was there as a stark reminder.

Rory did call her mobile that afternoon, but she didn't answer. His message was curt. She should contact him again only when she had stopped the escort work. It was immoral and he couldn't bear to think of her doing it. But he would at least see what he could do for her with the textile designs.

But her own misery was relegated to the back of her mind when she checked Kiki's emails. Her heart plummeted. There was one headed: HELP! It was obviously written in a hurry and sent before it was completed:

Tash, I've made a mistake. They've taken my phone and passport. Semy knows about this. I don't know how you can contact me, so I'd better leave it until

Natasha's mind was in a whirl. Where was Kiki? The email sender address ended in .cz, which was the Czech Republic. Natasha didn't know how she could find out for sure, but obviously she should get hold of Semyon immediately and drag the truth out of him. The man unnerved her, but she must do it for Kiki's sake.

She arranged to meet Semyon at Pushkin's that afternoon, on the pretence of finding out more about her escort date. The place seemed deserted. There was a pungent smell of stale cigarettes, drinks and lingering damp. The place was lit by overhead strip lights and looked most uninviting, hardly recognisable as the place she had been to with Kiki's crowd. There was a whispering of voices coming from somewhere, so she called out.

'Natasha!'

The voice came from the upstairs gallery. Natasha looked up to see Semyon, and thought she saw the head of another figure too.

'I'll come down,' he called. 'Wait there.'

Despite her trepidation, Natasha knew she owed it to Kiki to do the utmost she could.

'Natasha, I think I will guess why you want to see me,' Semyon said, once he had joined her.

'You can guess?'

'You want to know what I know about Kiki?'

'Dead right, Semyon,' she said, with more assertiveness than she really felt. 'Where is she? Who are Leonid and the old man and that creepy woman? They weren't representing the Russian government, were they?'

'Not exactly, no,' he admitted, a hint of amusement in his eyes. 'You are correct. Although the Russian government has made good use of them at times.'

'Semyon, stop stringing me along!' she hissed, her anger rising. 'I want to know what's happened. Who are they, and more importantly, what's happening to Kiki?'

'Sit down, Natasha,' he said with infuriating calm. 'This may come as rather a shock. You understand?'

She felt her knees going weak.

'I'm afraid they are people that I owed money to,' he said. 'Quite a lot of money. You know I have a dealing business on the side, so to speak.'

She nodded, trying to control her feelings. 'You mean, dealing in coke and crack.'

He waved a hand dismissively. 'Let's not name names—'

'And who was that woman with them?'

'Did she have silver hair and smoke black cigarettes?'

'Yes, and she looked a real bitch,' Natasha said with feeling.

'Ah yes, as I thought, that is Mme Bukoshi.' Semyon nodded sagely. 'I did not know that she was there. She has many contacts in Eastern Europe. This could be a good lead.' He paused and looked slightly over his shoulder, clearly sensing the presence of someone that Natasha had not. 'Now, I want you to meet someone, Natasha.'

Semyon smiled mysteriously at her as a shadowy figure appeared behind him. 'This is Jan, Natasha,' he said. 'He is your date for tonight. He thinks he can help you.'

Chapter 8

The Museum of Dance Education was not exactly a welcoming building. A long, almost windowless façade lay behind a high iron-barred fence in the historic Lesser Town. This was the area where the Renaissance nobility and the clergy built sumptuous palaces and churches, Natasha discovered.

Looking up, she could see the Hradcany outcrop, dominated by Prague Castle and the twin steeples of St Vitus's Cathedral. As she walked in through the dark portico, she shivered at the contrast and wished she were up there instead of here.

On a beautiful morning in early spring Natasha should have felt her spirits lift, but despite having spent almost a week in one of Europe's most romantic cities, Natasha felt sick with fear of what she was about to discover. As she waited with Jan in the vaulted marble foyer of the museum, surrounded by life-size bronze statues of scantily clad girls striking poses, she reflected on how things could have taken such a turn.

Jan came across as a model of charm and helpfulness when they had met at the nightclub a week before. Semyon had introduced him as the owner of a fine art printing business in Prague, but this was not entirely true. Jan told her on the flight over, with a boyish smile that anticipated her disapproval, he was actually a representative for two or three printing establishments that paid his expenses to visit western European publishers. But that was the least of his evasions.

Although Jan had assured her he knew where to find Kiki, he had not yet had any success whatsoever. Jan had paid for her fare and put her up in a smart hotel frequented by the international business set, but as he admitted sheepishly, running one hand through his wavy golden locks that were obviously his pride and joy, it might take some time to track down her friend.

So there she was, Natasha told herself trying to remain calm, staying in a beautiful city with time on her hands. In theory she could return to London at any time, since she had an open ticket, but the reason she was there was to find Kiki. She had printed the email message and given it to Jan, but there seemed to be no way of identifying the sender, even though the suffix identified the Czech Republic as the country of origin.

Or maybe Jan just wasn't telling her everything, because Natasha realised by the second night of her stay that her flight and accommodation bills were not going to be entirely free. Jan, knowing her escort experience, made it clear that she was expected to provide services on demand if she was to stay on in the hotel.

And already she'd had to receive two gentlemen. One had been perfectly charming and taken her out to dinner, but the other guy, an American, had threatened to rough her up if she didn't give him sex. She ended up bent over a chair with her jeans around her ankles as he took her roughly from behind.

She asked Jan how he was progressing with his enquiries, but what he told her nearly always included the words 'Mafia' and 'very secret', usually accompanied by a rubbing together of thumb and finger under her nose.

But at last, that morning he had found out that Kiki was working at the Museum of Dance Education, and told Natasha to go with him quickly.

As they drove through the narrow streets of the left bank, then through the Malostranska dominated by the baroque dome of St Nicholas, Jan explained to her about this strange place of detention.

It used to be a famous academy for dancers, he told her, with an attached museum. But since the mid-nineties the state was unable to continue funding it. Czech dance students preferred to go to Western Europe, where they could pick up better paid jobs. So, under the privatisation programme, it had been sold and was now, behind its sober façade, an upmarket bordello with some special tastes catered for. Oddly, the museum still opened for bona-fide visitors and researchers during the day.

Mme Eva was always on the lookout for western girls who had a more open mind on taking part in acts of depravity, and Jan had heard on the grapevine that through the Bukoshi woman Kiki had ended up there. He had phoned earlier to confirm this, and was told they might be able to see her. Natasha's excitement at the prospect of seeing her friend again was tempered by the awful thought of what state she might be in. She couldn't see Kiki fitting willingly into such a place. If they had taken away her passport and mobile, she must be there under extreme duress.

A severe-looking middle-aged woman shook Jan's hand, but Natasha wasn't introduced. She spoke briefly to Jan while looking Natasha up and down. Even though it was worlds apart in size and grandeur, somehow the place reminded her powerfully of the Academy.

They entered a long corridor with waist-high windows along one side. It was like an enclosed balcony from which there was an uninterrupted view into a series of large practice rooms, and a sumptuously panelled space with ropes and rings hanging from the ceiling.

Natasha was tempted to ask for information, but Jan indicated with a smile and a finger to his lips that this was not the time. He explained they were to be granted an audience with Mme Eva, who was the new owner of the museum. If she hoped to be able to see Kiki she must do exactly as Mme Eva said.

The woman flung open a pair of enormous doors at the end of the corridor and they entered a vast room, the lightness and elegance of which took Natasha's breath away. On three walls murals in ornate plaster frames stretched up to the ceiling, and a circular ceiling medallion showed dancers in the style of a Greek urn. Through the tall windows on the fourth wall light streamed onto the pirouetting ballerinas in the murals, and also lit up several Rodin-style male and female figures in dark bronze.

In the centre there were two sumptuous sofas on an antique rug, and there Natasha caught her first glimpse of Mme Eva Zitek, her dark shingled hair and long aristocratic face looking perfectly at home in the surroundings. This time Natasha was also greeted. The housekeeper retired, but remained posted in front of the double doors.

Mme Eva motioned for them both to sit opposite her, and poured two small glasses of green liquid. Her English was inflected, but much more idiomatic than Jan's.

'Natasha, this is Jindrichiv Hradec, one of our national drinks,' Mme Eva said crisply. 'You probably know it as absinthe. Have you tried it before?'

'No, but I don't really like strong-tasting spirits. Even though I'm from Scotland I don't even like the taste of whisky.'

Mme Eva gave her an encouraging smile. 'Then would you like a fruit juice?' she asked. 'We have some delicious fresh fruit crushes. Apricot? Grape? Minka, Hroznový džus pro Natasha.'

While Minka was away getting her grape juice, Natasha tried to work out what was being said. Although she thought she heard Kiki's name being used, she could make nothing of this harsh language which seemed to have no vowels. Everything was strange to her. Even the expressions on people's faces seemed unfriendly, yet no one had been anything but kind to her, as far as she could tell.

A glass of dark red juice was held before her and she took it. It was thicker than she had expected, with a wine taste, but she felt refreshed for it, and suddenly very relaxed.

'Now, Natasha, you have come about your friend, Miss Kiki?' the woman confirmed. 'Jan has told me that you are concerned about her safety.'

Natasha nodded eagerly, feeling she might at last be getting somewhere. 'We are such close friends, you see, and she hasn't been in touch for more than two weeks.'

'Quite.' The woman nodded stiffly. 'You are a loyal friend, Natasha, and that loyalty will be rewarded very soon. Now drink up. We shall be going behind the scenes at the museum, so to speak. We do not know yet whether this is the same girl as your friend, so we have not told her of your visit. You understand?'

Mme Eva asked her more questions about her background, and as she answered, Natasha felt her attention drifting and was suddenly very tired. Then she heard a voice beside her – a voice she recognised. She turned, and gasped with shock.

'Hello Natasha,' the newcomer said. 'I just knew

we'd meet again, didn't you?'

It was Phoebe!

Natasha hadn't seen or heard of the petit punk girl since the previous summer in Edinburgh! But here she was, standing before her in a strange place in a strange country, a look of despising etched on her face.

Suddenly, and without warning, Natasha felt her light dress being unbuttoned down the front as Phoebe fixed her with the eyes of a hypnotist. She protested ineffectually, but soon she was swooning with the dreamy pleasure of having her breasts stroked, and Phoebe was mocking her inability to resist. Then she was naked, sitting in front of the punk girl, who seemed to have changed in some indefinable way. Why had she allowed herself to be undressed with so little resistance?

She heard the clink of a chain, then felt her hands being manacled. She started to panic, and Phoebe, mocking her with laughter, held up the key just out of her reach. It was horrible. What on earth was going on...?

'Natasha, wake up!'

Why was Phoebe telling her to wake up? She tried to collect her thoughts.

'Please, Natasha!'

Through drowsy mists Natasha realised it wasn't Phoebe's voice. It was Kiki!

She opened her eyes and immediately cringed, clamping them shut again to keep out the harsh light. Her head was spinning. She felt nauseous, realising she must have been drugged. As she groggily opened her eyes again and raised herself up on one elbow, she saw that her wrists were manacled to the bed. Someone was helping her, and turning her head painfully she saw that it was indeed her friend.

Kiki babbled at her. 'Oh, Natasha, you're okay,' she gasped. 'Thank heavens! I was getting really worried. You looked jaked. Minka just brought me in here to identify a new arrival. I had no idea it would be you.'

It all came back in a rush. The visit to the museum with Jan, the splendid reception room, the fruit juice, and then the vivid dream. Now she was in far from splendid surroundings, more like a cell, with one small window high up, a grimy basin, and a narrow metal bed. She was wearing a plain blue gown and not much else, and there was no sign of her mobile phone or her bag containing her passport.

Kiki brought her water in a plastic mug.

'Kiki,' she managed, her mouth still dry even after a sip of water, 'this is a brothel, isn't it? White slave trade stuff. Semyon traded you to that Bukoshi woman through Leonid because of drug debts.'

Kiki nodded, and said miserably, 'I know.' She looked down and her shoulders began to shake. Now the two of them were incarcerated in the dreadful place. It catered for – what was Jan's phrase – some 'special tastes'. Natasha shivered in fear, but reached out for her friend, as far as she could in the manacles.

'I'm so sorry, Natasha,' Kiki sobbed, looking up at her friend again. Her eyes were blood-shot, with dark bags beneath them. She looked gaunt, her hair untidy. The sharpness and vivacity that Natasha associated with her were no longer there. She was also wearing a dark blue regulation shift.

'So, what are we going to do?' Natasha asked. 'What have you learnt from the other girls, Kiki? What exactly do you do here?'

'I've only been here about a week,' Kiki told her. 'To begin with Mme Eva trusted me, and I even helped her with her website. She left me alone for a few minutes and I managed to send an email, or at least half a one, because I heard her coming back.'

'Yes, I picked it up, but you didn't leave any address. So I had to use a Czech friend of Semyon's and, thanks to him I'm... anyway, that's not important now. Tell me what goes on here.'

'Well, the honeymoon period with madame didn't last very long. Just until I refused her sexual advances, to put it bluntly. So, for the last three days she's handed me over to Minka. She's the housekeeper, I suppose, a tough bitch who has a serious personality kink, as I've recently found out. Look at this.'

Kiki unbuttoned her shift and lifted it off her shoulders. Her lower back and thighs showed purple blotches, clear evidence of a recent beating. Higher up were fainter marks like dotted lines. Natasha's blood ran cold, partly at the signs of such severity, but also at Kiki's noticeable loss of weight.

'Kiki, whatever happened?' she asked sadly. 'What did she use to do that?'

'A bullwhip,' Kiki said frankly. 'A huge black thing made of plaited leather. I couldn't believe it when she suddenly produced it. Two Germans were there watching, at least, I thought it was just to watch. I don't know if I can tell you any more, Tash. It was so humiliating, and it was all Semyon's fault.' Her eyes brimmed with tears.

'Try to give me the full facts,' Natasha urged gently. 'Come on, girl. Remember, you were always telling me I was the oversensitive one.' She reached out to hold Kiki's shoulder, the manacle making her movements cumbersome. Kiki sniffled, and then started again in a trembling voice.

'Mme Eva told me that the clients wanted to watch a lesbian show. I was with Marketa, a Czech girl. I remembered what we two did together in London, so I thought it wouldn't be too bad.'

She took Natasha's hand and held it in a tight grasp.

'But it was nothing like that, Tash,' she whispered, the memory making her fight to hold back the tears. 'We stripped each other. It was in one of those practice rooms that you probably saw from the corridor. Lots of bare wooden floor, so we did it on a mat. I should have realised that this was where the client came to watch the punishment sessions. I think Marketa knew. Jesus, I'm such a numpty sometimes.'

Kiki went quiet and gazed up at the ceiling, her eyes sparkling with moisture. Natasha squeezed her hand for encouragement. 'Come on, Kiki,' she said, 'tell me. I'm not going to hold it against you. Your head's all mixed up thanks to your habit. But we'll get away from here and I'll help you sort yourself out. I promise.'

Kiki took a deep breath, and then exhaled heavily. 'Well,' she eventually continued, 'after we'd done a bit of foreplay, up comes Minka in her usual surly way, holding a length of cord. In her broken English she tells us to stand together, facing each other. She ties the cord four or five times around our waists and then underneath between our legs, fixing it with a knot at my back. She was grunting as she did it, and chatting away with the two Germans. They seemed to find what she was saying amusing.

'So there we were, both nude, tied tight and whispering encouragement to each other. Then Minka produced the bullwhip.

'I remember Marketa started to whimper, saying, "No, No!". I tried to think of some way to calm her. But then I heard the crack of the whip just by my cheek, and I nearly jumped out of my skin. Minka shouted for us to stand still. I was struggling with the knot with one hand behind my back, but the bitch saw that and caught me a vicious blow. I'd never known such pain, and was convinced it must have cut me. A split second later Marketa's eyes narrowed and her mouth opened without a sound as I felt her buttocks twist to the crack of the whip. Then, after a few more, I got the same treatment, right across the buttocks, sometimes on the back.

'I could see it was Minka's speciality. My inner thighs are still tender and, here, look at my wrist. Tash, there was nothing we could do to escape it. It was terrifying. We couldn't make any movement. And anyway, if she missed one of us she'd catch the other.

'After a few minutes she curled the whip up into several loops and held it in one hand, then inspected what she'd done. I imagine she was well pleased. By now one of the Germans had stripped, but even then I didn't realise exactly what was about to happen...'

Kiki jumped, and her flow was interrupted by the sound of a key turning in the lock. The housekeeper came in with a suitcase that Natasha recognised as hers. Jan must have brought it from the hotel after leaving her behind in a drugged stupor, and she suddenly realised exactly what lay behind his friendliness! Jan knew all along that he would be able to get a good price for her from Mme Eva. He had even charmed her out of one of the more risqué photos from her book, and with that he would have been bargaining with Mme Eva all the time she was stuck in the hotel. And she was earning him more money, no doubt, from entertaining the businessmen in her room. She certainly didn't get much from them. The bastard! She and Kiki had been treated shamelessly by men they had trusted.

The housekeeper dropped her case with bad grace. She indicated, as she unlocked the manacles, that Natasha was to wash with the soap and bowl of cold water provided in the corner, and dress to have dinner with Mme Eva. She leered at her as she reluctantly obeyed, licking her lips lewdly.

Once washed, Natasha opened her case and selected a dress, its plain simplicity enhancing her innocent beauty. If she could charm madame a little, however abhorrent the prospect might be, it might just work in their favour.

This time Mme Eva received her in a more intimate room, with an ornate marble mantelpiece over a log fire, even though the evening was mild. A light cold supper was laid out on a small mahogany dining table. In the middle was a candelabra, the only light in the room, which was once again lavishly decorated with ornamental plasterwork. Mme Eva was dressed in governess style, with a high-collared blouse fixed at the throat with a jade brooch. She offered Natasha some wine.

'Is it safe?' Natasha said sarcastically.

Mme Eva chuckled, her eyes sparkling in her intelligent face. Suddenly Natasha realised just how hungry she was, and couldn't ignore the delicious selection of cold meats and smoked trout, with a refreshing salad full of olives and pimentos. As she ate, prompted by Mme Eva, she gave an edited account of her recent life, hinting that she knew important people. After they had finished eating Mme Eva moved to a chaise longue, upholstered in burgundy velvet. She patted the space beside her encouragingly.

'Now, Natasha,' she said, 'I think it is only fair to explain why you are here at my museum.'

'I would be interested to know, and for how long I am expected to stay.'

'But that will depend on how well you work while you are here. I have had to pay for you, as you probably realise, so you must earn me enough to make the deal profitable. I have to pay the upkeep of this beautiful place, so I am doing the Republic a favour, don't you think?'

'I suppose so,' Natasha agreed, although she wasn't really interested in the economics of the situation. 'But how long will it be?'

'Well, it will be months rather than weeks.' She held up a hand to silence Natasha's objection. 'While you are here, and if you are obedient, you will eat well and I can ensure you will have as many drugs as you wish.'

'But, madame,' Natasha said, finding it difficult to be nice to the woman, but knowing it was vital to be so, 'I can't spend time here indefinitely, and neither can Kiki.'

The woman thought for a while, her eyes devouring the lovely girl sitting meekly beside her. 'Perhaps,' she said at last. 'It is all a matter of trust. Such a thing has to be constructed slowly. I thought your friend Kiki could be trusted, but she disappointed me.'

She stood abruptly, her perfume wafting around Natasha.

'Have you seen our beautiful city?' she said, completely changing the subject, confusing Natasha all the more. 'Come, I will show you.'

For a moment Natasha's heart leapt; perhaps they were going for a drive or something, providing her with a chance to escape. And then she could alert the authorities and arrange for Kiki's release.

But no, they climbed two flights of stairs and then some spiral stone steps that took them up to the roof. Madame unlocked a small wooden door and they stepped out onto a narrow walkway behind the roof parapet.

The river Vltava lay far below, the famous Charles Bridge with its line of statues all lit up and reflected enchantingly in its dark waters. Behind and above lay Prague Castle, silhouetted against a glorious sunset. There was only a slight breeze, and the noise of those sampling the streets at night drifted up to them. It was a bewitching scene, and Natasha felt herself becoming tearful, loneliness gripping her insides. This was so unfair; why was she being denied her freedom?

Mme Eva slipped an arm around her waist, the warmth of her body passing easily through her black skirt. Natasha tried to stay calm. This would be a test of her resolve. She had to stay on the right side of the woman, so she sighed resignedly and rested her head on her shoulder.

Even as Mme Eva turned her into her embrace, Natasha was making a rapid assessment of the scene below. In front of the museum, behind tall ornamental iron fencing, was a large area like a parade ground. The main gates were both closed, but during the day they would be open, like when she'd arrived with that snake, Jan.

She simply had to escape, even though she had no idea who she could turn to if she did. And without her passport how could she leave the country?

Natasha looked into Eva's finely chiselled features, made more prominent by the last rays of the dying sun. Eva smiled and, taking the girl's face between her hands, kissed her gently but lingeringly on the lips. Natasha tried to submit, but she loathed the corrupt harridan for what she was doing to her and to her friend.

'It's getting cold up here,' the woman said hoarsely. 'Let's go back to the dining room, my pet.'

Eva was a vigorous lover, as Natasha discovered as soon as they returned to the warmth of the room. The remains of the dinner had been cleared away and the fire was burning brightly. On the table were several mysterious bottles, small Venetian liqueur glasses with silvered rims and a matching water jug, all on a silver tray. The madame held up a squat green bottle.

'Maybe you remember this?' she said. 'Again I offer you the absinthe, Natasha, and this time I insist you will try it for my sake. It is a very Czech drink. We say you have to taste the bitter to know the sweet things of life when they come. Try it, my sweet. I promise it is not drugged.'

She deftly added water and the absinthe turned cloudy. They stood facing each other, and the woman tossed her drink to the back of her throat, and held it in her mouth. Natasha lifted the glass gingerly to her lips, and took a cautious sip. She coughed, the drink biting her throat, her eyes beginning to stream. Was it poison? Fear flashed through her mind, and then, just as suddenly, the taste invaded her mouth and she felt an intense wellbeing. She knew there would be the repeated shock, but she sipped once again, this time retaining the drink in her mouth before swallowing. The aftertaste made her giddy.

Eva guided her over to the chaise longue, and as she went Natasha felt her dress being stealthily unzipped from behind. Then she obediently stepped out of the dress and turned to sit on the velvet seat, reaching behind her to unclip her bra and release her breasts. She dropped the garment to the floor, then lay full length, one elbow on the backrest, dressed only in black panties. Strangely, now she was almost naked, she no longer felt threatened.

Mme Eva handed her the glass to finish while she retired behind a beautiful tapestry screen in the corner. Soft music played. Natasha drained her glass and relished once again the flavour of the drink. Then she stood up to return the glass, and saw Eva watching her from behind the screen. Standing close to the fire, she slowly and provocatively slipped out of her final garment, watching the woman's haughty expression soften into desire.

When Mme Eva stepped from behind the screen, she was a very different figure. Gone was the Victorian governess; instead she had become a firebreathing dominatrix. A scarlet waspie and elbow length gloves in matching satin made a startling impact, but Natasha's gaze was rooted on the jutting black phallus that Eva now sported at her crotch. Without taking her eyes off Natasha, she reached behind her to tighten one of the nylon straps.

Natasha backed away, the fragile confidence instilled by the drink instantly evaporating. She bit her lip and tried to steady her nerves. Following the woman's unspoken demand, she reached out gingerly to take the squat black member in her hand. It felt rubbery, and softer than she had imagined it would, but it was cool to the touch.

Eva reached out and grasped a handful of Natasha's hair behind her neck, forcing her head back and taking her waist in her other hand to pull it towards her. Then she kissed the girl hard and long, making Natasha gasp for breath as the woman forced her tongue into her mouth. Eva pulled her hair tighter, wrapping a turn around her fist. Again she kissed her fiercely, her mouth open. Soon Natasha's breasts were being mauled by Eva's long fingers.

Eva stopped kissing her, but kept a firm hold of her hair. She turned her round and stood close behind her, touching her stomach softly, then moving inevitably down to her sex.

'You must learn to do everything I ask, like the other girls,' the woman whispered hypnotically. 'Your role in this place is to submit to me and do exactly what I tell you to do. I am your mistress, do you understand?'

'Yes, madame...' Natasha acquiesced, 'but please be gentle with me.'

'Gentle? But why?' she scoffed. 'Jan has already told me that you are experienced in making love with a woman. You and your friend Kiki, no?'

'But, we only did it once,' Natasha protested pitifully.

'No more than once? He told me you had done it many times. I should have guessed. That Jan will not be trusted by me again.

'Now,' she continued, 'reach forward and kneel on the chaise longue. You will not be hurt. Just do as I say, Natasha, if you want me to treat you kindly.'

The experience was one Natasha would never forget. All memories of little Phoebe and her initiation into the delights of lesbian masturbation were swept aside by Eva's muscular lovemaking. Madame Eva retained her hold on Natasha's hair, tugging it whenever she wanted the girl to arch her back more and submissively present that silken purse for ease of penetration. Then madame stood between her legs and, after a breathless pause, during which she gazed down imperiously, relishing the sight of her delicious prey, inserted a cool finger between Natasha's sex lips, massaging them until gloriously wet and receptive. Only then did she thrust with her hips, gently at first while getting the angle right, but with increasing force and rapidity.

Such was the strength of her attack that Natasha soon found her cheek forced up against the back of the rhythmically creaking chaise longue, her head turned uncomfortably to the side. She could not counter or deny the authoritative woman's will. And despite everything she was becoming desperately excited, as from the corner of her eye she could see Eva's vigorous efforts as she rutted against her bottom.

Against her will Natasha reached her first orgasm, but still the insistent rhythm continued, driving her into a frenzy. Natasha tried to twist away from her oppressive grasp, but she was pinned against the furniture, with little room for manoeuvre. Her hair was tugged as if she were a horse being reined in. The aggressive thrusts continued unabated. Now they were accompanied by slaps across her buttocks. Natasha realised she was being sucked into the woman's rhythm, the ripples of pleasure heightened to unbearable levels by the energy of her. Natasha realised she knew her sexual responses as only another woman could. Eva thrust again and again with her rigid member. Her face was glowing in the firelight. Would she never tire?

Eventually Eva groaned, rested her weight on Natasha's back and slowly withdrew. She unstrapped the glistening dildo and dropped it to the floor. Then, sinking onto the red velvet seat next to Natasha's sprawling figure, she began to pleasure herself, her eyes tight shut, and within mere seconds she had worked herself into a state of simpering ecstasy.

When it was over she hugged Natasha's exhausted body, and even asked if she'd enjoyed herself. Natasha, aware enough to see the glimmer of an opportunity, asked if she could have a supply of cocaine to see her through the next few days.

'Of course you may, my dear,' the woman cooed maternally. 'I will instruct Minka and you will be given some tomorrow morning.

'Now,' she went on, 'you must find your way back to your room. Do you think you can do that? I think you should sleep well. Be quiet, as everyone else should be asleep.'

The quietness of the corridor, with sounds of sleepers from behind doors, reminded Natasha of the Academy. To the outside world this was, after all, just a museum with a dance academy attached.

Natasha slept fitfully, to be woken by Minka shaking her shoulder. She held a clear plastic packet in front of her face. Natasha took it and rubbed her eyes, and the next minute she was jerked awake as the sheet was stripped off the bed and she was pulled into a sitting position, told aggressively to get downstairs for breakfast, and then the loathsome housekeeper stomped out.

Dressing quickly and tying her hair up, Natasha was ready. She wanted to go with Kiki, but she didn't know which room she occupied. So she followed another blonde down to what turned out to be the basement kitchen. She helped herself to fruit and yoghurt and joined four or five others at the large scrubbed table. There was a cooking range against one wall, making it stiflingly hot in the kitchen, but the windows were closed.

'Hi, I'm Natasha,' she said, and to her relief the

others greeted her with a show of friendliness. Only two, a German and the Czech girl Marketa, spoke any English. They all seemed lethargic, but Natasha put it down to the heat.

'Why don't we open a window?' she suggested.

'Oh no, that is against the rules,' Marketa told her. 'A kitchen window is only open when there is a member of the staff in the kitchen. At night it is locked.'

'Why?' Natasha asked.

'It is just a rule,' said Beate, the German girl. 'As you can see, there are no bars on the windows, so we could all escape, couldn't we?'

'Except we do not have passports or identity cards,' Marketa added dolefully.

'So who is in charge of the kitchen?'

'It is Minka. She is in charge of everything.'

There was silence for a while, as the girls ate their breakfast.

'Do you know my friend, Kiki?' Natasha asked.

The girls nodded, and looked at each other without speaking.

'Is she coming down for breakfast, or should I take some up to her room?'

'She won't want it,' Marketa told her. 'She never eats until later in the day. Besides, she is ill this morning from too many drugs last night. She blacked out.'

Natasha was stunned, but Marketa smiled at her reassuringly.

'Don't worry,' she said, 'she has done it before. The doctor will call later to check she is okay.'

Natasha knocked gently on Kiki's door. Getting no response, she pushed it open and entered a small room almost identical to her own, except that a curtain was drawn across the high window. Kiki stirred, groaned, and turned to face her.

'Oh, it's you, Tash,' she said feebly. 'I thought it was Pavel.'

'How are you feeling?' Natasha asked gently.

'Apart from my head feeling like a landmine, I guess I'm not too bad. They tell me I took too much of a snort yesterday. God, my head!'

Natasha brought her a glass of water and sat down on the bed. Close up, she realised how haggard Kiki looked. And there were broken veins visible all over her face. How could she possibly continue to work here without her health giving way entirely?

'Is Pavel the doctor?' she asked. 'Surely he must realise you can't go on staying here?'

Just at that moment there was a knock on the door and Minka came in with the doctor.

'Hello, Miss Kiki, you have been a very bad girl again, I hear.' Despite his greased-back hair and pencil moustache, Natasha felt comforted when he smiled at her. Although American accented, his English was good. He said something to Minka, which made her retire to the door, then he opened his bag and checked Kiki's heart and lungs.

Natasha watched him, realising with a sick feeling that this was likely to be her only chance. She had to do something. The doctor shook his head and gave her a worried look.

'Is she your friend?' he asked her. 'You must try to get her to stop taking the drugs. Her system is becoming weakened.'

'But how can she stop in here?' Natasha said desperately. 'They give her free drugs every day.'

Pavel pulled a personal organiser out of his jacket pocket and flipped open the lid, checking the dates in his diary.

'Can you email on that?' she asked innocently, an idea suddenly forming in her head. She didn't want to arouse Minka's suspicions by whispering, but she had to keep her voice hushed. 'It's our only chance of getting out of this place,' she said, sensing she could trust the man. 'Please help us.'

But it was as if Pavel hadn't heard. He summoned the housekeeper and requested something, and her stern expression softened, obviously delighted to be taken into the doctor's confidence in this way.

As soon as she was out of the door, Pavel was on the alert. 'So you have the address of someone I can email?' he said conspiratorially. 'I can do that for you, but no more, you understand?'

Of course she did, but oh, whatever was Rory's address. Her mind had gone blank. Any minute now Minka would return and the opportunity would be lost.

Then she remembered something else. They had added his email address as a link on Kiki's website just last week when he was staying with her. Pavel was eyeing her anxiously.

'Well?' he urged. 'We must be quick. Here is my card, but do not let Minka or Mme Eva see it. It would not be worth the risk for me to do anything that harms Mme Eva. She is a powerful woman in this city.'

Natasha had to remember Kiki's web page. 'Look,' she said, 'there's a link on a website I'll give you to a Rory McElhone. I'll write it. Do you understand?'

'Better, key it into the organiser, and give me a message to send. I will try to send it out this evening when I get back to my surgery.'

Hastily she started keying in the message, fearing Minka's return at any moment:

Rory I'm in Prague and in terrible trouble. You can communicate with Pavel. Kiki is ill but I cannot get her out. Please help us.

She heard returning footsteps. She must think fast. She shook Kiki's arm, to get her attention.

'Kiki,' she hissed urgently, 'what's the address of your website? Kiki, come on, quick. It's our only chance.'

'What?' mumbled Kiki, looking at her friend with bleary eyes. 'How do you mean?'

'Kiki, just believe me, okay? I need it this very second.'

As Minka came in with a tray Natasha got to her feet, ostensibly to make space on the bed, but really to give herself a pretext to turn her back and key in the address. Minka looked at her suspiciously, but she turned round and held the palmtop behind her back.

Pavel was explaining to Minka the dose that Kiki was to receive, and as he did so, Natasha noticed he had one hand behind his back too, the fingers waggling to attract her attention. Understanding his silent signal, she carefully switched the black instrument to him, and almost fainted with relief as it was slipped into his pocket. Now all she could do was pray he would find the links to Rory's email address.

That afternoon Natasha was summoned once more to Mme Eva's reception room. She was wearing the regulation shift in dark blue, knee-length with white ankle socks. Her other clothes were still in the suitcase, which she had hidden under her bed. For some reason Minka had forgotten to come back for it, but it could surely only be a matter of time before she remembered.

Two particular guests were expected that evening, she was told by madame. For Natasha to know what was expected of her she must accompany the woman to watch.

'I think you are worried for your little friend,' she observed. 'She is so stupid, taking too many drugs. We have tried to ration her, but it is no good. The doctor says she is very sick. You must warn her that our patience is, how do you say, running short.'

Mme Eva sighed as if the cares of the world were on her shoulders. Her flashing eyes narrowed, her aquiline features a mask. Natasha shivered. She sensed that Kiki was in very real danger, and not just from the drug habit.

'Here, my sweet, but you are a comfort to me,' the woman said, breaking in to Natasha's worried thoughts. 'Let me hold you. You are obedient, unlike the other girls. But they must learn that they will be punished for it.'

Mme Eva beckoned for her to sit at her feet. She toyed idly with her hair and reached down to gather it up.

'You know, with your hair up like this you could easily be mistaken for a Slav. You have the eyes and the face bones.'

'Cheekbones,' Natasha corrected without thinking. 'My parents were from Lithuania, madame.'

'Ah, I guessed there was something different about you as soon as I saw your picture. So unlike your friend, Kiki. I bought her on trust from Mme Bukoshi. Now I am unwilling to release her until I have made her earn back some money. If only she could arrange herself better for a few weeks at least, then possibly... perhaps you could talk to her, Natasha.'

After leaving Mme Eva's suite she went straight to

the kitchen, where she was to help the cook prepare the evening dinner. Once again she checked out the windows, which were now open. The afternoon was hot and the sun poured in. The windows were high, but Natasha was sure that by standing on a box or two she could reach the ledge and pull herself through. She could then reach back, hopefully, and pull her suitcase after her. She would have to negotiate the drop to the ground on the outside, but then she would be in the courtyard and within touching distance of the outside world.

The problem would be getting her suitcase into the kitchen and finding somewhere to hide it. She looked in briefly on Kiki, but she was asleep, so she left her a note.

In the kitchen she saw that she and Beate were down for helping prepare breakfast in the morning, so, over the supper table she decided to explain to Beate her escape plans. She had hoped to talk to Marketa, who would know the nearest metro station to get her to Pavel's. But the blonde was nowhere to be seen, and Beate curtly explained the situation.

'It is her turn tonight,' she said. 'She will have nothing to eat before going down to the dungeon. That is the wisest thing.' Beate refused to elaborate, but she said she would help provide Natasha with an opportunity to conceal herself in the kitchen the following morning.

After supper she joined a group of girls who went up to Marketa's room to help her prepare. Apparently Mme Eva was already entertaining the guests in her reception room.

Marketa was being brave, Natasha could see. Others there had been in the dungeon before, but this was her first time. She was wearing a white tunic rather like a night-dress, that buttoned up the front. Her blonde hair was brushed to her shoulders and she wore simple sandals. It was like the garb of a penitent.

Natasha wondered if she knew how she was to be punished, or even for what, but didn't like to ask. She felt uncomfortable, knowing that later she would be spying on the events in the dungeon.

And what she saw numbed her to the very soul. Mme Eva had arranged a two-way mirror in a small cubby-hole that contained a few chairs, and a videocam on a tripod. She called it her Training Room.

She turned the light down and sat next to Natasha. Then at the touch of a button on a remote control the curtain drew back to reveal the events taking place in the dungeon. Two men stood in the centre of the gloomy space, both wearing elaborately coloured gowns with hassocks. Another figure dressed from head to toe in black leather rose from a golden throne, and Natasha realised it was Minka.

And there was Marketa! She was kneeling on the stone-flagged floor, naked, her wrists bound together behind her back with studded leather cuffs.

'Now watch closely,' Mme Eva whispered, as though merely enjoying a movie at the cinema. 'That bad girl is about to receive her punishment. This you will have to learn to endure when you make a mistake – as you certainly will.'

Mme Eva put a hand on Natasha's thigh and stroked her through the rough material of the gown. Then the two men helped Marketa to her feet, and Minka knelt to fix her ankles with similar cuffs.

The two men took her arms and leaned her backwards, while Minka brought a large hook attached to a length of rope. The hook went through rings in both pairs of bracelets, and then Marketa lay on her side in a foetal position, joined at wrists and ankles.

Then Minka motioned for the two men to haul on the rope. Immediately Marketa's limbs jerked upwards, folding her body as she rose jerkily into the air. Her face was turned to one side, and Natasha felt the poor girl was looking directly at her through the two-way mirror.

No time was lost. Minka began to twist Marketa round and round. Then she instructed one of the men to hold her steady while she slipped into the shadows, and then a sudden beam of light cut through the gloom to hold Marketa's pale body in its bright shaft. Minka appeared again, brandishing a range of implements of punishment, most of which were discarded on the throne. Then, gripping a long broad strap of leather, she nodded at the man holding Marketa. He let her go, allowing her to twist ever faster in one direction, and then more slowly in the reverse direction. Whichever way it was, Minka lashed out with the strap and soon the girl's slim body was covered with blushing patches.

Then a padded bench was brought over by the two clients. Marketa's wrists were released and the two hooded figures lowered her to an almost horizontal position, and the strap was handed to the other man. He threw off his cloak to reveal a fine physique, and a mass of black hair spreading from his shoulders down to his belly, where a pair of boxer shorts was his only garment. His companion retained a hold of the rope, by which means he could raise or lower Marketa's legs and buttocks.

'Are you enjoying this, Natasha?' Mme Eva, her eyes still glued to the scene before them, was unbuttoning Natasha's shift, and Natasha tried not to cringe.

'I think poor Marketa is suffering too much,

madame,' she said. 'I hope for her sake this won't continue much longer. What has she done to deserve it?'

'She must have been disobedient, don't you think?' the woman mused.

'Have I been obedient, then?' Natasha asked timidly.

'Why do you ask?'

'Do I deserve more cocaine as a treat?'

'All right, my darling,' the woman said. 'But promise me you won't turn out like your friend Kiki.'

Natasha raised a brave smile as a thank you, but when she looked through the mirror again she nearly cried out with dismay. Marketa was caught once more in the bright beam of light, hanging free of the floor, but now by her ankles alone. Her arms hung down as if she hoped to reach the floor and support herself, but there was little chance of that. She twisted and jerked like an eel, her hair hanging down and concealing her face. And as she twisted both men lashed at her with riding crops. Occasionally she would raise her torso for a moment of supreme effort to try and save her back from further punishment.

'Madame, please stop this,' Natasha pleaded.

The woman smiled wolfishly at her. 'Will you come to my bed then, my Natasha, after the guests have departed?'

'Yes, yes,' Natasha blurted without thought. 'Only stop it now, please.'

Mme Eva laughed and ruffled her hair. She pushed another button and immediately on the other side of the glass Minka pressed a finger to her ear. She glanced towards the mirror and nodded. She stepped forward and, looking at her watch, indicated to the clients their time was up. Then the curtain moved back to obscure the disconcerting scene.

That night, after she had left Mme Eva's bed with a promise of a hundred grammes of cut cocaine, Natasha hardly slept.

Beate knocked on her door at around six in the morning. She held out a small backpack, and Natasha hugged her. This was the missing link. She could foresee real problems about getting past the gatehouse with a suitcase, whereas a backpack would make her look just like an everyday tourist. She packed it with as many clothes as possible and the two stashes of cocaine.

Neither Marketa nor Kiki were at breakfast, and the news was not good about either of them. Kiki had hardly stirred from her bed for two days, and Marketa was recovering from her ordeal.

After breakfast Beate and Natasha were left with the cook to wash up. It was only a matter of a few seconds while the cook was out of the kitchen for Natasha to hide in one of the large pantries. Through the thick door she heard Beate speaking to the cook before leaving. Was she being betrayed? No, the cook was going about her tidying up. Now Natasha just had to hope and pray she wouldn't be discovered before the cook locked the kitchen until lunchtime. She tried to hold her breath to increase the sharpness of her hearing. There was the noise of pots being hung up on hooks, and the undertone of the cook's tuneless humming.

Then another nerve-wracking silence... and eventually the sound of the key turning in the lock of the kitchen door.

Natasha slipped from the pantry with a pounding heart. She could hardly believe the kitchen was empty. She piled up and climbed onto three milk cases, and managed to open the window. Climbing down again she quickly changed out of her blue shift and into jeans and a singlet.

It was now or never!

Natasha climbed up to the window again, dropped the rucksack out, hauled herself astride the window ledge, and dropped down to the ground with an agility that surprised even herself. She guessed she had, at best, about two hours before the kitchen was opened again and her escape discovered.

Retrieving the rucksack, she peered around the corner of the building. There was her goal, but her spirits plummeted as she saw the main gates were closed. Filled with despair she was wondering what on earth she could do, when she noticed the door to the gatekeeper's kiosk was open. It was a gamble she simply had to take.

The thirty metres or so of dusty courtyard she had to cross seemed like so many miles in the hot morning sun. And as she got closer to the open door the more unlikely any of her hastily put together explanations began to seem. Not that the gatekeeper would be likely to understand much English, anyway. If he didn't recognise her she might be able to bluff her way out as a visitor. Otherwise she would just have to stall for as long as possible until tourists started gathering at the gates and she could make a scene.

But to her immense relief and amazement the kiosk was empty. She could walk right through to the outside world! It was like a dream. She didn't know whether to laugh or cry, such was the intensity of her relief.

As she emerged into civilisation beyond the gatehouse she thought her legs would crumble beneath her. Such was her excitement and anxiety she couldn't breath, and keeping her head and eyes fixed firmly to the front, not daring to look back, she gradually broke into a trot, and then a run, and she fled the awful place as quickly as she possibly could.

Chapter 10

Even as she ran, Natasha's mind was also racing wildly. In the crowded streets of the Lesser Quarter, already becoming hot in the morning sun, she would probably lose herself. And how was she to find Pavel without help?

And how was she to get enough money to feed herself and find somewhere to stay while achieving her aim of rescuing Kiki? Without her passport, not only was she unable to exit the country, but she couldn't even change her traveller cheques. They, apart from a few crowns and a twenty-pound note, were all the money she had.

To make some cash she would need to trade the small bags of powder she had cajoled out of Mme Eva. That had always been her plan, but dealing she had never done before, and she had very little idea how to go about it. And it was something she was unhappy about, since it would put her in the same category as Mme Eva and those who had fed Kiki's habit. Glancing continually over her shoulder, Natasha walked quickly and tried to think calmly.

There were so many uncertainties. Had Rory received her message via Pavel's palmtop? And just how bad was her friend? She must try and find answers as soon as possible by contacting Pavel. But at all costs she must avoid being recaptured.

Her course was taking her up to the Hradcany outcrop. Soon the twin gothic steeples of St Vitus towered above her, shimmering in the heat. She stopped to get her breath; although the backpack wasn't heavy, the exertion of her fast pace uphill had left her dripping with sweat. Natasha was tempted to sit on a wall to rest, but she feared someone might be following.

She would seek some shade in the cathedral. A tremendous press of people was trying to get in, and Natasha realised that it was probably time for the morning mass. Inside it was cool, and the organ music was calming. She found a seat near the back and rested. She must have drifted off, because the next thing she knew someone had gripped her shoulder from behind.

Ahead the priest was standing in front of the high altar and people were queuing in the aisle for the host. Natasha yelped and, without daring to look back, wrenched free, grabbed her rucksack and squeezed her way along the row of seats. Her heart was still galloping as she burst out through a side door into the bright sunlight.

She was in a huge paved square and in the distance, as her eyes adjusted, she saw a troop of guards in feathered helmets marching in slow motion towards her. Was she dreaming again? An old man said something, beckoning her, but it seemed like a warning. So she ran away, under an archway and down a flight of steep stone steps. They were interrupted every so often by landings which gave access to the tenements on either side.

Suddenly Natasha knew where she was. In front of her, under an archway, lay the river Vltava and, more importantly, the famous Charles Bridge with its line of statues on each parapet. Somehow, by crossing this bridge where pavement artists and trinket sellers abounded, she felt she was returning to normality, away from the nightmare world of the museum.

In the Old Town the streets were much narrower. She tried to control her breathing and think clearly. She knew it was around here that Pavel lived and, to her immense surprise and relief, with the aid of directions, she found the flat that doubled as his home and surgery. But her relief was cut short when a severe-looking woman, either his housekeeper or his mother, answered the door and communicated with only the barest English that he was away all day and maybe the next, too.

Natasha was devastated. How could she have got into this dreadful mess? It was now mid-afternoon and she was exhausted by the stifling heat and lack of food. She spent several precious crowns on a fruit drink and hunkered down in an entrance to relish the can's coolness. A girl of about her own age with a bag over her shoulder smiled at her as she went in, and a couple of young men followed a minute later. More and more people were arriving. Natasha looked more closely at the notice board beside her. It read:

Ta Fantastika Black Light Theatre – visit our very special Czech mime theatre.

A matinee performance was about to start. Entering, Natasha saw the friendly girl at the box office. She began to explain how she had no money, but the girl put a finger to her lips and slipped her a ticket. Gratefully, Natasha went into the small theatre. It was dark, and the performance was just beginning.

When her eyes had adjusted to the light she could

see that brightly coloured cartoon fish were swimming back and forth across the stage. Suddenly a girl in an old-fashioned bathing costume was swimming as well. It was strange, unreal. Natasha felt like a child wondering at how the illusion was done, but not wanting to lose the sense of wonder.

In the next scene the girl was flying over a cut-out of the Prague skyline. She was dressed in a white dress and straw hat, rather like Alice in Wonderland. There were clowns who did impossible somersaults in slow motion. It was mesmerising.

Then the scene changed to an interior and the girl was in bed. A frightening bat-like figure came swooping in through the window, making Natasha gasp. Suddenly she realised this was like the recurring dream she used to have when she lived with Jim. Like her the girl was also naked. She was swept up into the air by the vampire figure. The bright colours and disconcerting figures were so similar to her dream that Natasha sat rooted to the spot. She was a child again, and being bewitched by the party magician.

But unlike her dream, here innocence triumphed and the evil forces retreated into the darkness they had materialised from. As the performers took their bows Natasha realised how it was done. Figures dressed head to toe in black manipulated the cut-out characters, and the human characters were on wires or supported by invisible hands.

Natasha applauded enthusiastically and wanted to say how much she had enjoyed it. The girl from the box office was standing at the back, so Natasha began to talk to her, but she wasn't really understanding. Then she touched Natasha on the forearm and beckoned her to follow.

She was taken along a corridor and into a tiny

room that served as a dressing room for the female cast. A girl with long blonde hair greeted Natasha, and she realised it was the girl who had just played the Alice figure.

'Hi, I'm Janis,' she said warmly.

'Hi,' said Natasha. 'I was just trying to tell her,' she indicated the sweet girl from the box office, 'how much I enjoyed the performance.'

Janis smiled appreciatively. 'That's nice of you,' she said. 'I'm so glad you liked it. Are you on vacation?'

Natasha hesitated slightly, and then said, 'Kind of... well, not really. I'm desperate to find somewhere to stay tonight. I lost my passport, you see.'

'Oh, that's dreadful.' Janis seemed genuinely concerned. 'You'll have to report it to the British Embassy and get a temporary one. How did it happen?'

'Well, it's not lost exactly. I, well, you see, I know who's got it.' Then, infuriatingly, she burst into tears. Finding someone who offered sympathy and wasn't out to exploit her made Natasha's heart melt. She thanked Janis for the tissue she gave her.

'Well, you needn't worry about somewhere to sleep tonight, Natasha,' Janis declared brightly, trying to cheer her up. 'Come and stay in the women's hostel where I'm based.'

Janis explained that she was free that evening because another mime artist and she took it in turns to perform. She was an American who had come to Prague specially to work with Black Light theatre, and she was drawing only enough wages to pay her accommodation, but luckily she had a generous allowance from home. Natasha had learnt all this and more during four stops on the metro.

The hostel was in a similar type of converted palace to the Museum of Dance, but with a much more open prospect overlooking a garden square. Waving aside Natasha's objections, Janis said she would pay for her room for a week, so she wouldn't have to worry. Natasha felt the tears springing to her eyes again, and squeezed the bubbly girl's hand with real affection. Never before had she warmed so much to someone in such a short period of time.

The next morning Natasha slept late. She sat up and looked around at the pink walls and the miniature white furniture, and for a moment she wondered where she was.

Then she jumped from bed, washed, and got dressed; valuable time was being wasted. She had to try and get in touch with the doctor again, both to hear if Rory had been contacted and also to find out about Kiki.

With the help of a passer-by and much arm waving, she soon rediscovered the correct street and was standing outside the door with the brass plaque, having rung the bell, praying he would be back.

The door opened and the surprised face of Pavel greeted her. Glancing anxiously up and down the street and quickly ushering her inside, he explained that he had been away at a conference, but had returned late the previous night. To Natasha's immense relief and joy there was an email waiting from Rory demanding details of her whereabouts, and Pavel had given the address of the dance museum, not knowing she had escaped from there.

'That's okay, Pavel,' she said. 'I was so afraid you wouldn't find Rory's address. Now at least he knows what's been going on. I'm sure he'll come.'

'It is possible,' Pavel agreed. 'But I must go now,

Natasha. I have just received a call from the museum. Mme Eva says your friend Kiki has become worse. She is trying to deprive her drugs, but she is becoming violent, you understand. I must go quickly.'

'And I must come with you,' Natasha said, her concerns for Kiki increasing with the news.

Pavel shook his head. 'No, no, you stay here with my wife until I am returned with news about your friend.'

'No, I have to see if I can find a way of getting her out of there,' Natasha insisted. 'I just have to try to do something. Kiki's my best friend, and I'm the only chance she's got so I have to do what I can to help her.'

She arranged to travel in the back of the car, keeping well down as Pavel swung in through the gates of the museum and parked well to one side of the building. Luckily, there were a number of cars already parked.

'Remember, Natasha,' he said, without turning back to look at her, 'if you are taken you must not tell Mme Eva it is me who bring you here. She is powerful and could make my life very difficult indeed. So, you understand the situation? If you take my advice you will wait here. Then see when I return with news of your friend Kiki.'

He grabbed his black bag and left Natasha hidden in the car. What should she do? She looked at the dashboard clock to see that it was four o'clock. The museum would close in half an hour. After that the main doors would be locked. If she managed to sneak in she might be able to see where the keys were kept, then later she and Kiki could make their escape during the night.

She had to try and do something; she remembered

how Kiki had helped her escape from her disastrous relationship with Jim, and how she had helped her make contact with Rory.

Natasha opened the car door and slipped out into the sunshine. She went in through the main door, calculating that Minka would not be around while the museum was open, and looked for a hiding place in the foyer from where she could spy on the curator as he locked up. She was sure the key was kept handy somewhere. It was needed to let in clients of Mme Eva's who arrived after the museum's official closing time.

Only a few visitors were left now. She must find somewhere quick before the elderly man came out to check everyone was away. Her gaze fell on a door handle in the elegant panelling behind a row of columns. Where did it lead? Or, even better, was it a place to hide?

To Natasha's delight it was a broom cupboard and, by leaving the door only slightly ajar, she could obtain a good view of the entrance.

But then she heard the fearsome voice of Minka, and almost immediately the door was wrenched open and the figure of the fierce woman stood before her, scowling belligerently as she took in the identity of the crouching figure in the cupboard. And then a slow, leering grin gradually split her ugly features and she cackled like an overweight witch.

'So, you are back,' she spat. 'Good, now I punish you.'

With surprising speed the woman grabbed Natasha by the arm, the vice-like grip making her grimace and shriek for mercy. She was hauled violently across the entrance hall by her tormentor, no clemency being shown, and she suddenly suspected that Mme Eva's favours had made her an object of envy to Minka, and now she was to have her moment of revenge. Natasha almost called out to Pavel, in the vain hope that he would hear and come to her aid, but she stopped herself in time, realising it would be better to keep him as a secret accomplice rather than blow his cover.

Minka dragged Natasha through the double doors that took them into the long passage leading to Mme Eva's reception room, and the prospect of a visit to the woman left Natasha in a state of panic. She was bundled along and, after Minka's knock, into the grand reception room. There were two smartly dressed men taking drinks with Mme Eva, and the woman's eyes widened with delight as she saw the struggling and cursing Natasha. One of the men smiled at her and whispered to his companion, and Natasha realised it was Leonid, the very rat who lured Kiki off to Geneva and then betrayed her!

'You bastard,' Natasha hissed, all worries for her own safety evaporating in the unexpected presence of the onerous man. 'Do you have no conscience? Young women are being drugged and tortured in here!'

But he merely smiled arrogantly at her and shook his head.

'Natasha, my dear,' Mme Eva said, 'how nice to have you back. You have been a very bad girl. I trusted you, but you betrayed me.' She nodded to Minka, and with a feeling of dread Natasha sensed an unspoken understanding between them, and watched the leer return to the hag's face.

Once again Natasha was grabbed painfully by the arm, and dragged from the room. Down stairs they went into the Stygian gloom, a door was thrust open, and she was bundled into the dungeon. To her right was the two-way mirror, reflecting the gloomy flickering from the candle sconces on the walls.

In the centre of the frightening room Natasha saw, with an ever-sinking heart, the stocks. Minka lifted one end of the jaw and, with practised ease, pulled Natasha's head between them by the hair until her throat was in the large central depression of the lower frame. Then she snapped it shut and fixed it with a pin.

With a cackle she shuffled away, and when she came back into Natasha's line of sight she held a pair of linked wrist cuffs, which Natasha recognised as the ones Marketa had been wearing when she watched through the two-way mirror. The image of the blonde girl suspended from the ceiling and spinning in the spotlight remained in her mind.

Minka threaded the cuffs around the wooden upright before securing each wrist, and said gruffly, 'There, girlie, now you are ready.'

The spotlights switched on, dazzling Natasha as she tried to look up, bent over with her neck clamped between the jaws. She waited, facing the two-way mirror, imagining Mme Eva playing the perfect hostess behind it, asking the two honoured guests just exactly what they wanted to see.

Why were they there? She tried to think what the reason could be. Could it be to do with Kiki? Were they taking her away somewhere? Maybe the reason for Pavel's visit was to see if she was fit to travel.

But her fevered speculation came to an abrupt ending. The door opened and Mme Eva appeared, rather bizarrely wearing a light headset and microphone, so she could communicate with the unseen watchers. Natasha felt totally powerless, numb at the prospect of what lay before her.

'Yes, I understand,' the woman said into the microphone, and then turned to Natasha. 'Now, my dear,' she said, 'listen to what I have to say. Minka is almost ready to administer your punishment, and my guests require that you be whipped. You understand?'

Natasha felt too sickened to respond in any way.

The woman paused for a moment, offering the girl a chance to speak, but realising she had nothing to say, she nodded at Minka. The brutish woman moved in and Natasha shrieked as her jeans were swiftly opened and tugged down her legs, and then her panties torn away and left to dangle from one knee. The stocks were turned on squeaky castors so that Natasha was sideways on to the blank mirror, set up for public punishment.

'You will count, girlie,' Minka ordered. 'Twenty strokes.'

'Please... no...' Natasha whimpered fearfully. Where was Pavel? Why wasn't he there to help her?

But then all thoughts of blaming someone else for her predicament vanished and she howled pitifully as the first stroke bit into her stretched haunches, the stinging receding only slowly.

'Count!' Minka warned.

'One...' Natasha sobbed.

And the strokes continued remorselessly, the virago pausing only to hear the count before swinging the strap again and again with spiteful venom. Through her tears and sobs Natasha wondered whether anything could be worse than the pain and humiliation of a public flogging.

Six more awful strokes and then it was over. As she stood, contrite and wracked with pain, Mme Eva was conferring into her microphone. 'Well, Natasha, how do you feel?' she asked. She was nodding in agreement with something said by the observers behind the glass. 'I hope Minka didn't hurt you too much. I think she might have been just a little over-enthusiastic.'

'It does hurt, madame,' Natasha said quietly, feeling the fight draining from her. 'Can – can I leave now?'

The woman laughed lightly. 'Unfortunately not, my dear. Our two distinguished guests have come for your friend, Kiki.'

'Come for her? Why?' Natasha demanded.

'She does not really fit in here. These gentlemen have agreed to take her with them to another place.'

'What do you mean?' Natasha was filled with dread. 'What other place?'

'That is enough questions, my dear,' the woman said, toying with the emotions of her prey. 'Now then, unfortunately for you your experiences here are not yet finished. My clients want to be sure that you are well secured before they depart from here tonight. I promised I would make sure of this.'

Natasha closed her eyes in fear and resignation. She should never have risked coming back. She should have stayed on the outside and reported Mme Eva to the authorities. What a naïve fool she'd been.

'You will stay down here for a while to consider the seriousness of your situation,' Mme Eva said. 'You were very silly to try to cross me, Natasha.'

Minka stood with her hands on her hips and smirked at Natasha's predicament, licking her lips with evident relish as she studied the imprisoned girls blotchy red bottom and thighs.

Mme Eva turned and faced the mirror, gave a little bow, and then turned back to Natasha. 'Now, you will remain down here until I decide otherwise,' she said coldly. 'And believe me, you will be here on your own for quite some time,' and with that, she walked gracefully from the dungeon.

Licking her lips, Minka took the opportunity for one last little treat, and stroked Natasha's scolded buttock flesh with both hands. Then, with a husky promise that she'd be back later when the rest of the house was asleep and they wouldn't be disturbed, she followed her mistress, slamming the door with a fearful finality, her cackling laugh fading as she climbed the stone steps to the house above.

It was intolerable. Natasha's initial panic at being left alone in the macabre cell turned to anger as she realised that, although Mme Eva and Minka had left the dungeon, anyone could be watching her torment from behind the mirror. She was in the spotlight, and could feel its warmth on her head. Natasha was determined not to give them the pleasure of seeing her cry.

How long would she be kept in such an abominable way? When she got out that woman would pay for treating her so badly. Her mind drifted, and she realised she was floating in and out of consciousness...

How long had she been locked in the stocks now? How long since the two hateful women had left her alone? Tears filled her eyes and meandered down her cheeks as loneliness gripped her heart, and thoughts of poor Kiki being taken away again filled her with fear. Would her friend survive without help? Would she ever see her again?

Her eyes closed...

Through swirling thoughts and images Natasha heard something familiar. She opened her eyes wearily. Why was her mind tormenting her so? How long locked in the cell now?

Then she heard the sounds again. It couldn't be

what it sounded like; she must be hallucinating. Then she stiffened, her eyes snapping wide open, and she heard screams... and raised male voices.

They were shouting, barking orders. There was Minka's voice, sounding strangely compliant. And then the voices were getting closer and footsteps were stomping along the main corridor above. One voice in particular seemed evermore familiar, and appeared to be English.

Natasha mouthed a silent prayer.

And then the door burst open, and there was no longer any doubt.

'Natasha,' Rory gasped, 'what have they done to you?'

Once she was free from the awful stocks and her jeans had been pulled up over her sore bottom, Natasha's first gabbled question was about Kiki's whereabouts and wellbeing. To her relief, Rory told her that Pavel had given the authorities the necessary information and they had acted to have Leonid's car stopped at the border. After receiving Pavel's message Rory had immediately emailed the authorities, and they had been keeping the dance museum under surveillance since. He had taken the next flight and arrived in Prague at about the same time as she had made her fatal mistake of returning to the place.

Upon storming the building they had discovered the other girls at work in the neighbouring dungeons and rooms, and now a police doctor was examining them all. There would be very serious charges brought against Mme Eva, and Leonid, if Kiki testified against him.

'The important thing is to reunite the two of you and catch the first flight home,' he said, giving her a peck on the forehead and a comforting cuddle as he helped her from the cell and up the stone steps. 'Do you think you'll feel fit enough to travel after a good night's rest?'

Natasha looked up into his eyes, her cheeks still damp and glistening with tears, and gave him a weak but cheery smile. 'As long as Kiki's okay too, you just try and stop me,' she said.

Other titles available from Chimera (all £6.99)

190138862X	Ruled by the Rod	*Rawlings*
1901388638	Of Pain & Delight	*Stone*
1903931614	BloodLust Chronicles – Charity	*Ashton*
1901388492	Rectory of Correction	*Virosa*
1901388751	Lucy	*Culber*
1903931649	Jennifer Rising	*Del Monico*
1901388751	Out of Control	*Miller*
1903931657	Dream Captive	*Gabriel*
1901388190	Destroying Angel	*Hastings*
1903931665	Suffering the Consequences	*Stern*
1901388131	All for her Master	*O'Connor*
1903931703	Flesh & Blood	*Argus*
1901388204	The Instruction of Olivia	*Allen*
190393169X	Fate's Victim	*Beaufort*
1901388115	Space Captive	*Hughes*
1903931711	The Bottom Line	*Savage*
190138800X	Sweet Punishment	*Jameson*
1903931754	Alice – Lost Soul	*Surreal*
1901388123	Sold into Service	*Tanner*
1901388018	Olivia and the Dulcinites	*Allen*
1903931746	Planet of Pain	*Bradbury*
1901388298	Betty Serves the Master	*Tanner*
1901388425	Sophie and the Circle of Slavery	*Culber*
190393172X	Saxon Slave	*Benedict*
1901388344	Shadows of Torment	*McLachlan*
1901388263	Selina's Submission	*Lewis*
1903931762	Devil's Paradise	*Beaufort*
1901388077	Under Orders	*Asquith*
1903931789	Bad Girls	*Stern*
1901388042	Thunder's Slaves	*Leather*
1903931797	Notebooks of the Young Wife	*Black*
1901388247	Total Abandon	*Anderssen*
1903931770	Bondmaiden	*Bradbury*
1901388409	Domination Inc.	*Leather*
1903931800	Painful Consequences	*North*
1901388735	Managing Mrs Burton	*Aspen*
1903931819	Bound for the Top	*Dean*
1901388603	Sister Murdock's House of Correction	*Anderssen*
1901388026	Belinda – A Cruel Passage West	*Anonymous*
1903931827	A Wicked Conquest	*Saxon*
1903931835	Odyssey of Desire	*Vale*
1901388549	Love Slave	*Wakelin*
190138814X	Stranger in Venice	*Beaufort*

All **Chimera** titles are available from your local bookshop or newsagent, or direct from our mail order department. Please send your order with your credit card details, a cheque or postal order (made payable to *Chimera Publishing Ltd*) to: **Chimera Publishing Ltd., Readers' Services, PO Box 152, Waterlooville, Hants, PO8 9FS.** Or call our **24 hour telephone/fax credit card hotline: +44 (0)23 92 646062** (Visa, Mastercard, Switch, JCB and Solo only).

UK & BFPO - Aimed delivery within three working days.
- A delivery charge of £3.00.
- An item charge of £0.20 per item, up to a maximum of five items.

For example, a customer ordering two items for delivery within the UK will be charged £3.00 delivery + £0.40 items charge, totalling a delivery charge of £3.40. The maximum delivery cost for a UK customer is £4.00. Therefore if you order more than five items for delivery within the UK you will not be charged more than a total of £4.00 for delivery.

Western Europe - Aimed delivery within five to ten working days.
- A delivery charge of £3.00.
- An item charge of £1.25 per item.

For example, a customer ordering two items for delivery to W. Europe, will be charged £3.00 delivery + £2.50 items charge, totalling a delivery charge of £5.50.

USA - Aimed delivery within twelve to fifteen working days.
- A delivery charge of £3.00.
- An item charge of £2.00 per item.

For example, a customer ordering two items for delivery to the USA, will be charged £3.00 delivery + £4.00 item charge, totalling a delivery charge of £7.00.

Rest of the World - Aimed delivery within fifteen to twenty-two working days.
- A delivery charge of £3.00.
- An item charge of £2.75 per item.

For example, a customer ordering two items for delivery to the ROW, will be charged £3.00 delivery + £5.50 item charge, totalling a delivery charge of £8.50.

For a copy of our free catalogue please write to

**Chimera Publishing Ltd
Readers' Services
PO Box 152
Waterlooville
Hants
PO8 9FS**

or e-mail us at
info@chimera-online.co.uk

or purchase from our range of erotic titles at
www.chimera-online.co.uk

The full range of our titles are also available as downloadable e-books at our website

www.chimera-online.co.uk

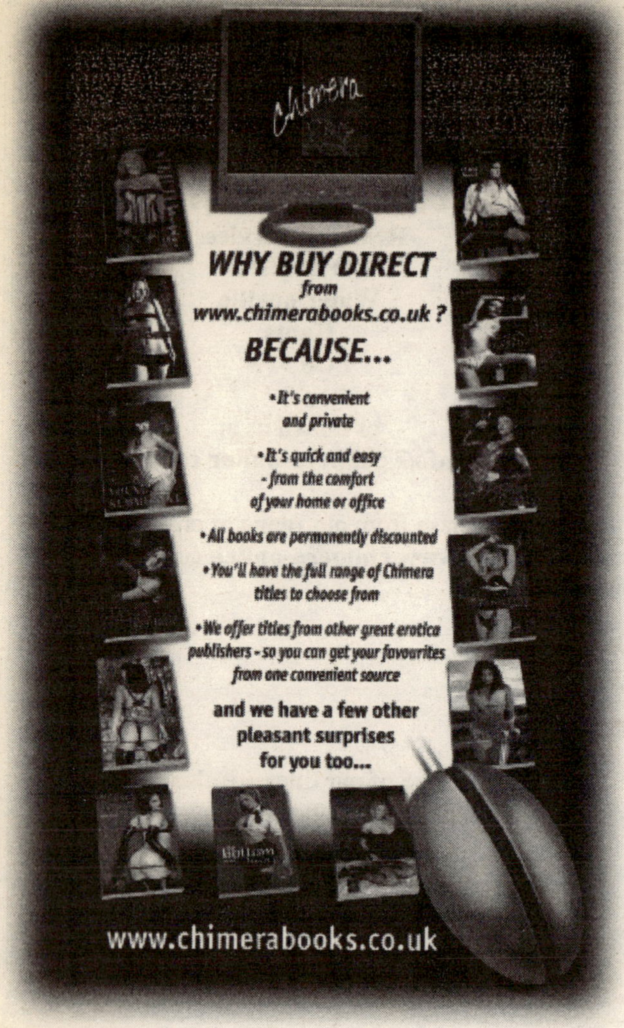
Chimera
WHY BUY DIRECT
from
www.chimerabooks.co.uk ?
BECAUSE...
•It's convenient and private
•It's quick and easy - from the comfort of your home or office
•All books are permanently discounted
•You'll have the full range of Chimera titles to choose from
•We offer titles from other great erotica publishers - so you can get your favourites from one convenient source
and we have a few other pleasant surprises for you too...
www.chimerabooks.co.uk